D0684047

ALSO BY JIM KNIPFEL

Unplugging Philco

Noogie's Time to Shine

Ruining It for Everybody

The Buzzing

Quitting the Nairobi Trio

Slackjaw

These Children Who Come at You with Knives, and Other Fairy Tales

JIM KNIPFEL

Simon & Schuster

New York   London   Toronto   Sydney

Simon & Schuster
1230 Avenue of the Americas
New York, NY 10020

Portions of Charles Manson's testimony on November 19, 1970, quoted from *The Manson File,* edited by Nikolas Schreck (Amok Press, New York, 1988).

First Simon & Schuster trade paperback edition June 2010

SIMON & SCHUSTER and colophon are registered trademarks of Simon & Schuster, Inc.

For information about special discounts for bulk purchases, please contact Simon & Schuster Special Sales at 1-866-506-1949 or business@simonandschuster.com.

The Simon & Schuster Speakers Bureau can bring authors to your live event. For more information or to book an event contact the Simon & Schuster Speakers Bureau at 1-866-248-3049 or visit our website at www.simonspeakers.com.

Designed by Jill Putorti

Library of Congress Cataloging-in-Publication Data
Knipfel, Jim.
 These children who come at you with knives, and other fairy tales / Jim Knipfel.
  p. cm.
1. Satire, American. 2. Fables, American. I. Title.
 PS3611.N574T47 2010
 813'.6—dc22   2009032151

ISBN 978-1-4391-5412-0
ISBN 978-1-4391-5900-2 (ebook)

Manufactured in the United States of America

10 9 8 7 6 5 4 3 2 1

For my nieces, Jordan and McKenzie Adrians.
Despite all my best efforts they turned out pretty damn good.

Yes, there is a hell my boy, and you don't have to dig for it.

—Jim Thompson, *Savage Night*

Contents

Preface:
World Without End, Amen

In the beginning was the Void. But it wasn't long before the Void started to lose its charm. I mean, what's so great about the Void? You stare into it, it stares into you, and that's really about the extent of it. Before you know it, it's time for a snack. Satan decided he needed something a bit more entertaining.

Using the finest materials he could create he fashioned himself a universe. Of the countless galaxies and stars and planets, he set one aside—one *special* planet, which would become his personal theater. This new and sparkling entertainment mecca he called Earth.

At first, Earth was nothing but a floating glob of molten rock so, after bouncing it from hand to hand until it cooled, Satan covered it with water and plants. Even after that, no matter how lovely the whole thing might've been, not a whole helluva lot happened on Earth. He soon discovered that plants and water alone were just as boring, pretty much, as the Void. Satan needed something more. A little action.

He took the materials left over from the creation of the universe and made some animals, which he then set loose across the planet. He made ocelots and platypuses and otters and gazelles and sleestaks and chickens and giant squids and gnats and triceratopses and vultures and bloodworms and fire ants and black bears and mastodons and stinkbugs and wildebeests. Then he sat back once again and watched.

The animals were awfully cute and amusing at first, but again in time he found that his need for uproarious, slambang entertainment remained unfulfilled. These animals he had created were too perfect. Their instincts were too refined and they were too self-sufficient. They used too much common sense in their dealings with one another and the world around them. If they wanted to eat, they found some food and ate it. If they were tired, they slept. There are only so many times you can watch a cheetah chase down a crippled antelope before your mind starts wandering and you decide to check out the Weather Channel again. What Satan needed was a new kind of animal—one that would remain unpredictable, whose entertainment value would not diminish with time.

Having by this point exhausted the last of his good building materials, Satan created these new creatures out of the shit his animals had left on the ground. It seemed to work well enough. Best of all, these new things stood on two legs, which increased their slapstick potential threefold. He decided to call these new creatures Man, for some reason.

Man was at first without senses, couldn't see, hear, taste, or smell. All they did was stumble around and bump into one another. Being made of shit, you see, they weren't very bright—though they were undeniably hilarious.

Satan looked upon his latest creations and thought, "Yeah, I suppose it'll do."

Unbeknownst to the others, one of these new creatures was different. He was slightly more clever than the rest—though only slightly—and as he bumped his way around Earth he learned things about his surroundings. One of the things he learned was that the other animals had special gifts that Man lacked. So one day he set about to steal their senses for himself and others of his kind.

Unfortunately, although he was clever in human terms, he still had shit for brains. He stole sight from the moles and smell from the birds. He stole hearing from the fish and taste from the dogs. Then he began distributing these fancy new senses around to his friends.

Satan watched all this and chuckled merrily. Humans at the mercy of their new senses were more entertaining than he could have imagined. He also appreciated their resourcefulness, for they reminded him of himself when he was young.

Knowing it was expected of him as the creator of the universe, he decided to pay a visit to the Earth one afternoon and confront the thief.

He found the thief in a clearing, testing out his new senses and giggling at his own cleverness. Upon hearing Satan's approach, however, he quickly pretended to be blind and deaf and halfheartedly began bumping into trees and rocks.

"Say," Satan said, feigning righteous anger as he entered the clearing and caught sight of his bumbling creation, "what's that you got there, Doug? *Senses?*"

"Umm . . . no?" the thief lied.

"Oh, c'mon now, Fibber McGee. Remember who you're talking to. You just *answered* me, which not only means you can talk, it means you *heard* me too. I mean, I'm not stupid, you know. I created the damn universe, after all. Let's see *you* do that." He folded his mighty arms and tried to keep up his poker face.

The thief, knowing the jig was up, fell to the ground and groveled at Satan's hooves, begging for his mercy.

"Oh, come now, stop that," Satan said, gently nudging the smelly thing away with his hoof. He liked these little dummies, and he wanted them to prosper, honest and for true. The last thing he was about to saddle them with was a nagging kind of guilt-ridden love. "Stop fretting. So you stole some senses. Big deal. Have I ever told you *not* to do anything?"

The thief ceased groveling for a moment and raised his dirt-smeared face. "Pardon?"

"Do what thou wilt, that's what I say."

The thief paused, confused. "Umm . . . really?"

"Sure! Whatever trips your trigger. Go for it."

"You mean it? It's not a trick?"

"Of course not."

"Woo hoo!" the thief yipped as he leaped to his feet, scampered away, and promptly jumped off a cliff.

Satan sighed heavily and shook his head. He then slowly strolled to the edge of the cliff and looked down at the prone, broken body in the ravine below.

"I didn't say 'Do what thou wilt, *stupid.*'"

He lifted the thief up, shook him back to life, and, with an affectionate pat on the butt, sent him on his way once more. Before doing so, he reiterated his only rule, adding, "But try not to be too much of a shit while you're at it." Then remembering where they all came from, he said, "Well, you know what I mean. Don't be an asshole."

Satan then returned to his den, poured himself a drink, sat back, and watched as Man created intoxicants, lawn furniture, money, fatty foods, aqueducts, neon signs, automobiles, other gods, poetry, intercontinental ballistic missiles, the electric chair, Smurfs, vaccines, deodorant, art, and sitcoms.

Most of them were indeed doing what they wanted. Some did wondrous things that surprised even Satan (sort of). Others did very bad things. They murdered and polluted and peed in the ocean.

Some arrogant, self-centered types divided the world into "masters" and "slaves." There were many more slaves than there were masters, but in a move that surprised the hell out of Satan, instead of banding together and beating the crap out of the masters the slaves turned being a slave into a virtue. They were suddenly proud of being weak, downtrodden slaves, claiming that being a slave was better than being a master, even building an entire religion around the idea.

"Well, whatever turns you on," Satan said, pouring himself another drink. "I don't get it, but there you go."

All in all, though, Man did okay for himself, and this pleased Satan. Despite destructive—and self-destructive—tendencies, they had some fun, too, and enjoyed many of the things that had been provided for them, like red meat. Some were remarkably intelligent, while a few ate poisons, put their eyes out with gardening tools, and drove their vehicles through store windows.

Relaxing with a cigar one evening, Satan thought, "This really is much funnier than I could have hoped for," and he was quite pleased. He found Man pathetic and clumsy and endearing, not unlike that three-headed puppy he'd made once by accident but decided to keep around anyway.

Some humans created grand things, like music and art and literature and science, all in an effort to understand life and make it better, and that was fine. Those who screwed it up, well, it was their own damn fault. Those who used things thoughtfully deserved the happiness it brought them. He wanted them to be satisfied with any and all available pleasures.

Satan wasn't much interested in being worshipped—he was comfortable enough with himself not to need that. He was happy just being an observer. Besides, he thought some of the other gods Man had come up with were delightfully silly, and he found high comedy in watching Man worship things in the most ludicrous of ways. Once a year, for instance, thousands of them got together and trampled one another to death during a ritual designed to celebrate one of these gods they'd made up.

"Tell me how *that* makes sense," Satan shrugged. But he didn't change the channel.

As the centuries passed, Satan noticed that not enough of these creatures were doing well. There was much sadness and despair and suffering among them. For being free to do what

they wanted with all they'd been given, most simply weren't very happy. A vague sense of disappointment seemed to accompany every action. Although this disappointment was Man's own doing, arising from expectations created by other humans, Satan felt he should intervene just this once to get things back on track. He went out to his garage and began working on a little gift.

A week or so later he visited Earth in order to bestow the orgasm upon his most beloved creation.

"Here," he told the collected masses as they gathered around him nervously. "This is for you." Then he winked at them. "You'll like it."

Man accepted the gift, but having been told over the years to be suspicious of gifts one of them raised his hand and asked, "What's the catch?"

"Catch?" Satan asked, playing innocent. "No catch at all." Then he grinned. "Oh, okay, you got me there. I confess," he said as he pulled a picture out of his bag. "There is one little thing." He held up the picture so they all could see it. "The catch is, when you use it, you'll look like *this*."

"*Gaah!*" the people shrieked, recoiling in horror.

They soon forgot about the terrible picture, though. Satan's gift seemed to make everything worthwhile, if only for moments at a time. All the pain, the suffering, the despair, and the doubt seemed to vanish. And that, Satan concluded, was the funniest and saddest thing of all.

These Children Who Come at You with Knives

The Chicken Who Was Smarter Than Everyone

From the moment she was hatched Gertie knew she wasn't like the other chickens. While they were perfectly content to bop around the barnyard like fuzzy yellow Ping-Pong balls, Gertie preferred to sit off by herself. She studied the behavior of the other chicks, stared at the sky, allowed herself to get lost in her own increasingly complex thought patterns.

At first, the other chicks barely noticed Gertie, who could often be found studying the discarded brochures and scraps of newspaper that occasionally blew through the yard. She was a little odd, they decided, but at heart just another chicken, and all chickens were the same. But as they grew older, they came to suspect and despise Gertie, who was more than simply odd—she was downright freakish and creepy and not to be trusted. She never talked to any of the other chickens, and she carried herself about the yard like she was somehow better than them.

This was not exactly true. Gertie simply thought there was much more to talk about than the weather and the latest tawdry bits of barnyard gossip. Who was this "Farmer Bernkopf," for instance, and what position did he hold in the universe? What was their true purpose there on the farm? The farm itself intrigued her as well. Was this the only farm in the universe or were there other farms beyond what they could see? Other farms with other chickens?

Of course when she attempted to bring up some of these issues with the other chickens, they laughed and called her "Poindexter" and "weirdo." Gertie soon learned that she had become the central topic in their cruel gossip sessions, which prompted her to stay even farther away from the other stupid chickens, joining them only at feeding time.

One day while exploring a corner of the farm she'd never visited before, Gertie noticed that the doors of an enormous, forgotten barn had been left open a crack.

The always curious Gertie peered through the open doors for a few seconds before squeezing herself inside. Then she stood still for a moment longer, allowing her tiny black eyes to adjust to the darkness.

Inside were mountains of books. Thousands upon thousands of them. History, science, literature, philosophy—books on all imaginable subjects, most of which Gertie had never heard of before. It seems that some years earlier, when the nearby Dub Taylor Memorial Library closed down for lack of funds, Farmer Bernkopf cut a deal to haul all the books away. Instead of carting them to the dump, as was expected, Farmer Bernkopf brought them home and stashed them in his unused barn. He wasn't much of a reader himself, the farmer, but thought he might get around to it one of these days. If that day ever chanced to swing by, he wanted to make sure he had something on hand.

Gertie was flabbergasted by what lay in front of her. She wasn't sure what the objects were at first but, upon examining one that had flipped open after falling off a stack, she understood what she had discovered. These were like the brochures and newspaper scraps she'd been reading, but they were filled with much more than announcements about "Two-for-One Sales," "Extended Layaway Plans," and baffling, incomplete accounts of what were called "football games."

Gertie was beside herself with excitement. She opened the first book, sat down on the straw-covered floor of the barn, and began reading.

Within the books she found the answers to so many of her questions and learned about things that were completely unknown to her, such as the Crimean War, particle physics, and automobile repair. More important, she learned that there was indeed an entire world beyond the confines of the farm. A magical world full of cities and jungles and alien creatures. There were even places called "universities" where questions like those Gertie had been asking her whole life were discussed openly and with great enthusiasm, where she would be able to engage others on her own intellectual level in a free and lively debate.

Once she finished reading all the books in the barn, she knew she had to get away. She burned with a desire to see this world she'd read so much about, and to visit one of these universities.

That night, she returned to the coop, packed up what few things she had in a small bag, and left without saying a word to any of those other stupid chickens who'd tried to make her feel like she was the awful one for not being just like them.

After hopping through a hole in the fence, Gertie walked and walked along the narrow clear paths that cut through forests and great, open farmlands. She felt a delighted tingle and a sense of freedom she'd not known possible. She felt, she thought, like Amerigo Vespucci.

One day shortly after she'd set out on her journey, a large hawk landed on the path in front of her.

"Hey there, chickie pie, where you goin'? You lost or something?" the hawk asked with a leer, convinced he wouldn't have to worry about dinner that night.

"No, I must say I'm not lost at all," Gertie replied. "You see, I'm on my way to fulfill my destiny. As Dostoyevsky once said about destiny—that is, the inevitable, inescapable conclusion of our actions in this life . . ."

The hawk, who considered himself pretty devious and slick, only stared at Gertie as she launched into a long lecture. His sharp black eyes soon glazed over and his wicked beak went slack. Before long, he fell asleep, and when Gertie finished her lecture she dragged him into the middle of the road and continued on her way.

The dirt road she'd been walking along soon became a paved, two-lane highway, and Gertie knew she was drawing closer to all the things she had read about. She knew all about the development of the American transportation infrastructure and its effect on the growth of middle-class suburban culture. She also knew about automobile fatality statistics, and so she walked far off the side of the road, just to be on the safe side.

While tromping through the underbrush one afternoon, she came face to face with a red fox.

"Hey there, sweet thing," cooed the fox, his mouth curling into a sinister grin. "You look like you might need a little help."

"Why thank you, no. I'm quite fine," Gertie replied. She tried to step around him but the fox blocked her path.

"No, baby," he purred, "you don't seem to understand. See, a big storm is headed this way, and I think it might be better if you hung out in my den until it passes. It's close by and you'd be safe in there. Why, I've even started a nice vegetable soup simmering."

Gertie, who knew all about the culinary habits of foxes as well as the complex mathematics at the heart of meteorology, peered up into the sky above them.

"A storm, you say?"

"Uh-huh," the fox replied, not taking his eyes off Gertie. "A big one. Just heard it on the radio. Thunder, lightning, who knows what all. Maybe hail too."

"Hmm," she said. "That's odd. Because given the nature of those clouds up there, the prevailing wind speed, and the currently steady barometric pressure, I'd have concluded . . ."

Off she went on another lecture, this one concerning the history of meteorology from Babylonian times through the mid-twentieth century.

Needless to say, the fox—like the hawk before him—was soon bored to sleep. Gertie again dragged him into the road and continued on her way.

The two-lane highway soon grew into a four-lane highway, and Gertie knew she was drawing still closer. There was more traffic speeding by and more billboards along the side of the road.

While passing beneath an enormous billboard advertising some new kind of bathroom air freshener, Gertie heard a voice call to her.

"Hey! Hey you! Chicken!"

She looked, and in the bushes beneath the billboard she spied the frightened face of an ocelot. This struck her as very strange, so she walked over to him. "I am indeed a chicken," she said, "but my name's Gertie."

"Fine, whatever," the ocelot said. He sounded out of breath.

"Well, I must say, for an ocelot you certainly seem to be far away from home. Thousands of miles, in fact, from your natural habitat. Are you heading to the city to find your destiny as well?"

"My destiny? Fuck no. I'm trying to escape."

"Escape?" Gertie asked, startled. "From what?"

The ocelot looked nervously over his shoulder and said, "Some fat bastard named Zimm . . . I'd been locked in that rotten prison of his for two years. It was unimaginably awful. He'd *torture* us. Every day he'd torture us—or have one of his machines do it. Electricity, cold, starvation. God . . ." The tears welled up in the ocelot's eyes. "And now he's after me with his dogs."

"Torture?" Gertie cried. "But that's illegal! Aren't they familiar with the dictates of the Geneva Conventions? It's quite clear. They aren't allowed—"

"Look," the ocelot said. "I don't know what you're talking about. All I know is that he was torturing us and that I got away."

"How'd you do that?"

"It's like this," the ocelot began. "One day, okay, I couldn't take it anymore. So I bit one kid—one of those rotten little monsters always poking at us with sticks and pulling our tails. It was just a nip, mind you, didn't even draw much blood, but the next thing you know I'm lined up for execution to keep the little shit's parents from suing."

"Execution?" Gertie exclaimed. "An ocelot?"

"Yeah, an ocelot. For one little nip. What the fuck do they expect? I'm a goddamn *ocelot*!"

"Indeed," Gertie nodded.

"Lucky for me they left me alone in the room for a minute, and I knew how to unlock the window. Next thing I know, I'm running for my life out here. It's been three days now and I think I might've finally shaken them."

"That's very good, then. Say, I'm on my way to the city. They'd never look for you there. And I bet an ocelot who knows his way around a lock could find all sorts of gainful employment. Care to come along?"

The ocelot, whose name was Stu, considered this for just a moment, then agreed. He didn't seem to have much of a choice.

"Along the way, I could explain the development of the polio vaccine, plus if we have time Eliot's poetics as they relate to his dramatic works."

Stu looked askance at Gertie and said, "Yeah . . . well . . . I guess I'll come along anyway."

"Very good, then. I'm so anxious to talk to people. And ocelots."

So on the two of them walked and walked, and before long they saw the skyline of the city in the distance.

Gertie (who had been talking almost incessantly) stopped, her tiny black eyes growing wide. "My goodness," she said. "Would you look at that? Why, I know now how Magellan must have felt."

"Yeah," replied Stu, who'd been fighting off the urge to smack the chicken a good one for the past two days. "Me too."

Once in the city, and right in the middle of a lecture on Louis Sullivan and the invention of the skyscraper—a particularly apt and interesting subject, Gertie thought—Stu made some lame excuse and disappeared down an alley.

"Just as well," Gertie sighed, as she watched him go. "He didn't have much to add to the discussion anyway."

She walked the streets, her beak agape and her eyes wide with awe. Wherever she went, people were talking and working and laughing. Everyone seemed so different. This was indeed where she belonged, instead of that useless barnyard with those dim-witted cackling hens. Such a stifling environment. It was amazing to her that she hadn't gone mad in all the years she spent there. It was so dry and hollow and dead.

The city, on the other hand, was vibrant and alive. There were words everywhere, and everywhere people were discussing important things: the events of the day, the fluctuating economy, the viable ownership of taxis. Many of the people she saw were announcing their locations into a small device most of them seemed to be carrying.

"I'm on Lexington and Fifty-eighth," they were saying, "and I'm walking north." Or, "I'm at the corner of Twenty-third and Seventh."

"There's so much whirlwind activity here," Gertie reasoned, "that it must be very important to announce where you are every few minutes, otherwise you might get lost."

She spoke to none of them, though. She had tried at first but was ignored. People stepped around her and continued on their way. For the first time in her life she felt intimidated.

She knew everything that was in all of those books back at' the barn, it's true, but those books explained the world as it was up until 1975, when the library had closed. Things had obviously changed a great deal since then.

Gertie knew what she had to do: she had to go to the university. There, they were less concerned with immediacy than with understanding the complex fundamentals of those things that have happened and may yet happen—the sciences, histories, literatures, and philosophies that crafted the world into what it was today.

So she walked and walked some more until she found the university. It was just as she had always dreamed it would be. Students carrying books, people discussing matters of Great Profundity. And the library! Why, the library contained a thousand times as many books as had been in the barn.

How should she approach this? Her immediate impulse was to become a student, to learn all that she could from brilliant professors and the eager, fertile imaginations of the other students. But how to do that? It would cost money, which Gertie, being a runaway chicken, certainly didn't have.

Perhaps instead, she thought, she could just sit in on classes without telling anyone.

She soon found a stained and discarded course catalog on a bench and began poring over the listings. So many of the choices excited her that she concluded she could stop into most any classroom on the campus and discover something valuable. So she set off to begin her formal education.

In the first classroom she visited, she found an elderly professor with a long white beard berating his students for their inability to construct a complete and coherent written sentence.

With a deep and sorrowful sigh, the professor said, "All right, I guess we have to start all over from the beginning. Again. Who can tell me what a noun is?" He waited expectantly, but the students only stared at him, dead-eyed.

"This certainly is not the place for me," Gertie thought to herself. "I would learn no more here than I would have if I'd stayed at the farm."

She went to another building and into another classroom, where a younger professor was lecturing on applied integral calculus. Or claimed to be lecturing on applied integral calculus, anyway. Mostly he was talking about baseball. He wasn't applying integral calculus to baseball either—he was just talking about baseball.

Once again, Gertie left the room in a huff. "If he wants to lecture about baseball, he should teach a class on baseball and drop the charade," she thought.

The third classroom was the final straw. During a single, hour-long lecture, an alleged professor of eighteenth-century European history made (by Gertie's count) thirteen blatant mistakes, yet he passed them along to his students as hard facts. Names, dates, locations—all wrong. And not just simple, innocent mistakes. *Big* ones. The group of dullards sitting in the lecture hall (who clearly hadn't done that week's reading) never questioned or corrected him. They just copied everything down in their notebooks.

Gertie, unable to contain herself any longer, finally blurted out from the back of the lecture hall, "I can't believe how wrong you are!"

The professor stopped in mid-sentence, and all the eyes in the classroom turned to focus on the chicken sitting in the back.

"Excuse me?" the professor said, his annoyance undisguised.

"First of all, mink farms did *not* represent twelve percent of France's gross national product in 1716. Second, Richard Wagner, who, mind you, wasn't born until 1813, was not inspired to become a composer after seeing a cartoon show, and third—"

"Hold on a second," the professor snapped, putting an abrupt halt to Gertie's tirade. "Hey guys," he said, addressing the students, "who are you gonna listen to? Me, the professor with the degree, or, like, a talking chicken?"

All the students roared with laughter and Gertie, believing neither her eyes nor her ears, stomped from the room in a fury.

"Idiots!" she thought. "All of them! Worse than those chickens!"

She was quickly growing discouraged. This was what passed for higher education? Ridiculous. Why, she could do a much better job than what she was finding here.

Then she had an idea. Why *not* do a better job? Instead of being a student, she should get a job on the faculty!

She marched over to the administration building and took an elevator to the office of the university president.

She walked into the office, eyes still blazing, and strode up to the receptionist's desk.

She hopped atop the desk and told the secretary, "I would like to see the university president, please."

The secretary stared at Gertie in shock. In all her years working here she'd never before encountered a talking chicken, let alone one who wanted to see the president.

"Um," she said finally, trying to be as professional as possible. "What is this concerning?"

"A teaching position," Gertie said. "I've just come from visiting several of your classrooms here, and what I saw was pathetic and dispiriting. I believe I could do a much better job."

"Oh," the secretary said. She hit the intercom button. "Dr. Varney?"

"Yes?"

"Talking chicken to see you, sir."

Dr. Varney was silent for a very long time. Then he asked, "What about?"

"A . . . a job, I guess."

"You didn't 'guess,'" Gertie told the secretary. "I told you. And that's exactly why I'm here."

"Oh," Dr. Varney said. "Well . . . send, er, it in."

A door next to the secretary's desk opened and Gertie walked into the president's office. "Take a seat, Mr. . . ."

"Mr.?" she asked. "Do I look like a rooster to you? My name's Gertie."

"Fine, I'm sorry. Take a seat, please . . . Gertie."

Flapping her wings wildly, she hopped into the large leather chair opposite his desk, found she couldn't see him, and so hopped upon his desk proper.

"Well," Gertie said, "as your secretary informed you, I'm looking for a position on your faculty."

Over the course of the next three hours, Gertie described her recent experiences in the classrooms, then went on to explain to Dr. Varney why she was more than qualified to lecture on nearly any subject, from French literature (in the original, of course) to anthropology, medieval history, non-Euclidean geometry, organic chemistry, and mechanical engineering.

When she was finished, Dr. Varney leaned back in his chair.

"Well," he said, "you certainly do make a strong case for yourself and your qualifications."

Gertie ruffled her feathers with pride.

Then he opened one of his desk drawers and pulled out three sheets of paper.

"Do you know what I have in my hand here?" he asked.

"Would it be presumptuous of me to believe that it's a contract?"

"Yes," Dr. Varney said, "it would indeed. No, Gertie, what I have here are copies of the Equal Opportunity Employment Act, the Americans with Disabilities Act, and the latest version of the Affirmative Action statutes." He laid them out on his desk for her to inspect.

"Now," he continued, "according to these, a man in my position, at an institution such as this, is obligated *by law* to hire a certain number of broads, cripples, and coloreds, got me?"

"Beneath the crude and offensive vernacular, I understand what you're saying, yes."

"Good. But please note that nowhere on any of those sheets of paper—and I encourage you to read them thoroughly and in detail—does it say that I am obligated by law to hire plump and juicy chickens, no matter how big a smarty pants they may be. In fact there's nothing in there about barnyard fowl of any kind."

"But that's a mere technicality," Gertie protested. "You're not obligated, no, but the fact remains—"

"Ah-ah-ah," Dr. Varney said, holding up a hand. "Now don't go giving me another one of those fancy speeches about the law and technicalities. My point, quite simply, is that, legality aside, I have no intention of adding a talking chicken to the faculty of this fine institution."

"I see," Gertie said, crestfallen. "Well, if that's it, then I'm sorry I wasted both of our time, though I thank you for agreeing to meet with me."

She turned to hop down off the desk when Dr. Varney said, "Now hold on there just a moment, little lady. I'm not quite finished yet."

"Yes?" Gertie asked, turning back to face him.

"I do know another fellow who runs an educational institution not far from here, one as equally prestigious as this one in its own way, and if I'm not mistaken—and I don't believe I am—he would be honored to add you to his faculty."

"Really?" Gertie said, her spirits rising again.

"Yes, really. In fact, why don't I just give him a call right now, see what we can work out?" He picked up the phone and punched a few numbers. As he waited, he gave Gertie a reassuring smile.

"Carl!" he barked into the phone. "Jack Varney here, and you're not going to believe this, but sitting on my desk right now I have the world's most brilliant chicken. Speaks several languages and is more than qualified to teach most any subject under the sun."

There was a brief silence.

"Yes," Dr. Varney said, "she speaks English. And French and Swahili. Her name's Gertie. Sadly, I don't have room for her here at the present, but I think she would be a fine addition to your institution. You better hurry on over, though, because if you don't snag her now someone from Harvard or Yale might, and it'll be your loss." There was another pause. "Yes, c'mon over. We'll be waiting for you."

He hung up the phone and said, "Carl will be here in fifteen minutes, depending on the traffic. I believe you'll be very happy with him. He's a man who takes great pride in the brilliance of his per . . . professors."

Gertie, delighted by this sudden turn of events, joined Dr. Varney, and the two of them went downstairs to wait.

Although Gertie was very wise in matters of book learning, she had acquired very little by way of real world common sense, and she had yet to realize that she shouldn't take what humans told her at face value. She was, in short, a very smart chicken but a very dumb cluck.

Ten minutes later, a black Oldomobile pulled up along the curb in front of the administration building where Dr. Varney and Gertie were waiting.

A beefy man wearing a cowboy hat got out and yelled, "Jack, you ol' devil!"

"Why hello there Carl, it's good to see you again. How's my sister doing?"

"Fine as ever, Jack, fine as ever. What can I say? She's quite a woman."

"Yes she is, isn't she? Well. Enough of the small talk. I would like to introduce you to Gertie, the chicken who's smarter than everyone."

Gertie extended a wing and Carl bent down to shake it. "It's a pleasure to meet you, Gertie."

"The pleasure is all mine, Carl. I hear there may be an opening for me on your faculty."

"Why, there just might be at that," he said. Then he caught himself. "No, forget *might*. I can say right now that in fact there is."

Gertie's heart leapt.

"If you'd like," Carl said, "we could head over to the campus right now and I could show you around, let you meet a few of the people you'll be working with."

"I'd be delighted," Gertie said.

After thanking Dr. Varney for all his kindness and help, she waited for Carl to open the door, then hopped into the front seat of the Olds. He slammed the door, got in the driver's side, and the two of them drove away.

"Where is the university?" Gertie asked. "You must be nearby, given how quickly you arrived."

"I must confess, I was very excited to meet you, so I may have exceeded the speed limit. But it's not far."

"This is all happening so quickly," she said. "I barely know where to begin. You know, it was only a few weeks ago that I was living on a farm with other chickens?"

"You don't say."

"It's true. But then I came to the city to find my destiny and"—she sighed deeply—"it's looking like I've done just that. I do believe I was born to teach."

"And teach you will," he told her as he took an exit heading out of town.

"Goodness me," she said, suddenly realizing something. "I'm afraid I'll have an awful lot of catching up to do." Then she added, "You'll need to excuse my occasional bouts of ignorance when it comes to contemporary history and figures of import. My own education took me only to a certain point. I still have so much to learn."

"Don't we all?" Carl asked. "But I guess that's why we're in the education business. It's not just students who learn, but we learn as well, I must say." He tipped the cowboy hat back with a finger. "Not a day goes by that I don't learn something. Take today, for instance. Before today, I never thought I'd ever meet a talking chicken, let alone one with a brain like yours."

Gertie blushed beneath her feathers. Then she looked out the window and began planning her first several lectures. The first one, she thought, would focus on pre-Columbian architecture.

"Yessir," Carl was saying, as the buildings fell away and the landscape around them grew flatter, except for occasional clumps of trees. "You will be a fine addition to the faculty. As Jack may have mentioned, I take great pride in the intelligence of my . . ."

Gertie was only half listening. There was so much to think about and see and plan. Plus she'd never ridden in a car before so there was that excitement, too, along with the thrill of seeing the landscape zip by so fast. The last thing she caught before Carl slipped into his own reverie was ". . . but I've never seen anything like you in all my days. And I'm trusting nobody else has either. Yessir, you're exactly what I've been looking for."

Twenty minutes later the Olds pulled into a long dirt driveway, which ran beneath a wooden sign that read ZIMM'S EDU-RIFFIC INSTITUTE OF FUN AND CHEESE EMPORIUM.

Not surprisingly, news of Gertie quickly spread far and wide, and every day people lined up by the hundreds to see her renowned brilliance on display.

Carl Zimm had given her a special glass box to live in. One wall of the box had been decorated with a large electric panel. The floor, too, was electrified. Being a lightning-fast learner, it didn't take Gertie long at all to get the hang of things.

When one of the people who stopped to see her inserted a quarter, the panel on the wall would light up with a display of large *X*s and *O*s. She could sometimes play as many as five hundred games of tic-tac-toe a day, depending on the crowd. And every time she won, which she almost always did, some feed corn would fall through a slot and the floor would momentarily cease shocking her feet.

In a box to her right, a white duck danced to the off-key tinkling of a toy piano for ten hours a day (encouraged by a similarly electrified floor). In the box to her left, a rabbit drove a toy fire engine around in circles. Both had long ago completely lost their minds.

The Boy Who Came to His Senses

Once upon a time there was a young man named Marvin, known by friends and family behind his back as "Marvin the Numbskull." Sometimes they forgot and called him this to his face, but Marvin didn't seem to notice.

Oh, he was a good-hearted lad, and he certainly wasn't stupid, but he had an awful tendency to get himself embroiled in troublesome situations without thinking them all the way through. More than once was the time Marvin, always smiling and oblivious, had to be bailed out by someone before he got his legs broken or was slapped with an eight-year prison sentence.

One summer evening during his eighteenth (almost nineteenth) year, Marvin was enjoying a few practice rolls at his favorite bowling alley, the Kegler's Kompound. It might not've been the fanciest bowling alley in town—the plastic seats were cracked, the rug was worn thin, and the air reeked of cigar smoke and rental shoes long past their prime—but Marvin was comfortable there. Plus, he'd been going to Kegler's for so many years that he'd found all the grooves in each of the lanes. These days his league played on Saturday nights, so he always liked to get at least three practice games in on Thursday or Friday to make sure he was loose and limber when it counted.

That night, however, he found himself distracted halfway through his first game. The most beautiful girl he had ever seen was bowling three lanes away. He couldn't help but try and steal a few furtive glances her way every time she stepped up to her approach. He noted that she was a four-stepper, just like he was.

She had flowing golden hair and the face of an angel. She appeared to be around his age. And built? You better believe it! Normally the girls who hung around the Kegler's Kompound (and there weren't many) looked like they'd been beaten with shovels.

More remarkable still, she appeared to be all alone.

Emboldened by his complete lack of guile as well as the adrenaline and hormones tickling his brain stem (those couple beers didn't hurt either), Marvin picked up his ball, his towel, and his score sheet and moved down next to her as she waited near the ball return. Three years earlier, even two, such a daring move never would have occurred to Marvin, but things change.

"Why, good evening," he said, as the sound of pins crackling and crashing echoed in the air around them. "Are you alone here this evening or are you waiting for someone?"

"I am indeed all alone," she said, her voice wistful and a bit unbelieving. Best of all, she didn't seem annoyed that he had spoken to her, the way so many other young ladies had in the past. More than once, such conversations had ended almost before they could even begin. Just a month earlier, in fact, one young lady at a bus stop let him know she wasn't interested by emptying a soda bottle full of bleach over his head.

"Well, in that case," Marvin asked, "would you mind terribly if I were to roll on this empty lane next to yours?" He may have been a numbskull but he was always polite.

"Please do," the young woman offered with a sweet smile. Her ball clunked and spun out of the return and she hoisted it. It was bright pink and looked to be a sixteen-pounder. Marvin was impressed.

Hardly believing his good fortune, Marvin placed his ball and score sheet down, then, after she returned from picking up the spare, introduced himself.

"My name's Marvin," he said, "and I'm very pleased to meet you . . . Ms. . . . ?"

"I'm Oswalda," the young woman replied.

"Oh," Marvin said, wincing slightly. "So . . . what brings a lovely young woman such as yourself to a shithole alley like this?"

After that incredibly insipid opening (and ignoring the hurt look on the face of the alley's general manager, who happened to be walking past at that very minute), the two youngsters all but forgot about bowling, sat down, and fell into a rambling but exhilarating conversation.

Much to Marvin's delight, he discovered that they shared many interests apart from bowling (though bowling was certainly a biggie). They were both interested in home appliance repair, seventies heavy metal, and curling.

"This is really something," Marvin thought to himself shortly before saying it aloud. "Imagine discovering a young lady—let alone one as lovely as this—who knows so much about curling."

Finally noting the annoyed glances from the manager, they each rolled a few frames to justify sitting there that long. Marvin was surprised at what a fine and seasoned bowler Oswalda was.

"Why, this just keeps getting better and better," he said to himself.

Things, incredibly enough, got better still around ten o'clock, when Oswalda suggested they return to her apartment. Marvin had to be to work at his dad's stationery store by nine the next morning, but this was an opportunity he simply couldn't pass up. He knew his dad would understand when he explained it to him.

The two packed up their balls and returned their rental shoes and stepped outside, where Oswalda hailed a cab with only the daintiest twitch of her delicate white finger. (It often took Marvin half an hour of jumping and yelling and waving his arms before a cabbie—mostly out of pity—stopped for him.)

The ride to Oswalda's place took twenty minutes, and along the way they continued talking about all sorts of things—their favorite amusement park restaurants, Louis L'Amour, the Japanese obsession with Colonel Sanders. When the cab finally pulled to a stop outside a beautiful and ornate apartment building in Chelsea, Marvin was quite awestruck.

"*This* is where you live?" he asked, staring out the cab's window, his eyes tracking up the building's facade.

"Yes, I'm afraid it is," she said, as if it were no big deal.

Marvin wasn't sure why he was so surprised to learn that a girl like this lived in such a high-zoot building. To look at her it

was clear she had a lot going for her. By contrast, most everyone else he knew—guys who had very little going for them—lived in rented garages or crummy cold-water flats in Queens and the Bronx. He'd never known anyone who lived in a palace like this.

Oswalda paid the cabby, and as they walked through the building's glass doors the doorman greeted her with a tip of the hat and a "good evening, miss."

Marvin and Oswalda rode the elevator up to the penthouse. When she unlocked her door and let him inside, Marvin was left nearly speechless by the opulence before him. Medieval tapestries hung from the walls and enormous crystal chandeliers glowed from the twenty-five-foot-high ceiling. Floor-to-ceiling windows offered a breathtaking view of the Manhattan skyline. The antique furniture was covered in silk and leather and the carpeting was the most luxurious he had ever stepped upon. There was no telling, from where he stood, just how large the apartment was, but it seemed to go on forever.

"My goodness," he said, "look at this place."

"What?" she asked, her voice filled with concern. "Is it filthy? I *knew* Grimalda'd been shirking her duties—"

"No, no!" Marvin explained. "Quite the opposite. I've never been in a place of such splendor before. Splendor *and* opulence. Never."

"Oh," Oswalda said, as if no one had ever pointed this out to her. "I guess it's okay. Nothing like my other place."

"Your . . . *other* place?"

"Oh yes, I have a couple floors in a co-op on the Upper West Side. I just came here tonight because it was closer."

"I . . . see," Marvin said. "Golly. And you live here all alone?" She nodded as she set down her bowling bag. His heart began to pound. He was really into something good here, that much was for sure.

"Take a look around if you like," Oswalda said. "I'll go get us something to drink. I'm parched." Then she left him standing alone, his eyes still wide.

Eventually he strolled over to the enormous fireplace. On the mantel rested a series of photographs in frames made of gold and diamonds. The largest photo was a portrait of a large man with a long red beard. He was scowling something fierce into the camera.

When Oswalda returned carrying the drinks and some elaborate snacks on a silver tray, he was struck again by how honestly good-looking she was, relieved to know it wasn't just the dim lights of the bowling alley that had led to his conclusion. He was nearly speechless for the second time in ten minutes. How could a woman this amazing be alone? Why wasn't there a line of guys much richer and better-looking than Marvin stretching down to the sidewalk? Why was she paying even the slightest bit of attention to him?

Finally, with some effort, he asked, "Who's this?" half-pointing at the portrait of the scowly fellow.

After she set the tray down upon the polished marble coffee table in front of the black leather couch, she turned to see what he was pointing at.

"Oh," she said, "that's my father, the king."

"Your father," Marvin asked, his throat tightening, "the *king*? You mean . . . ?"

"Yes."

"Your father's the *king*?"

"Uh-huh." She seemed almost too casual about this little fact.

"Guess that would explain the crown he's wearing. So . . . that makes you . . . ?"

"Yeah." She nodded shyly, seeming a bit embarrassed. "Princess Oswalda Vitamin."

"Oh," Marvin replied. "Um. Congratulations."

"Thanks. I don't like to mention the princess stuff too often. I try to keep it under wraps until I know I can trust someone. It just gets in the way otherwise."

"I can understand that," Marvin said, even though he didn't understand it at all. If he was a princess, why, he'd make sure the whole world knew.

Something she said struck him suddenly. "You—you mean you feel you can trust me?"

"Sure," she offered with another one of her sweet smiles. "I knew from the minute you stepped over to my lane. Unless of course there's some reason I shouldn't."

"Oh no," Marvin said, "not at all. If there's one thing I am, it's trustworthy."

"I knew as much. Now come over here and sit down. Have something to drink with me."

He was in a situation here that went way beyond simply *good*. This was astonishing. Overwhelming. Mind-boggling. Something that was completely unthinkable earlier that day. She was beautiful and bright. She knew her curling. She *bowled*. And on top of it all she was an insanely wealthy honest-to-goodness princess, for godsakes. He couldn't wait to tell his brothers. They'd be so proud of him.

They sat on the couch until shortly after midnight, talking and laughing. Marvin forgot about work the next morning. It was all quite perfect. And Princess Oswalda Vitamin seemed to be having a good time as well. It was almost *too* perfect. At last Marvin couldn't contain himself any longer.

"I'm not exactly sure how one goes about this when dealing with a princess," he began. "But I'm having such a splendid time. I know now that there is no other woman in this world for me. So what do you think? You wanna get hitched?"

"Oh Marvin!" Oswalda exclaimed happily. "I'm speechless. Why, I was sitting here thinking exactly the same thing."

"Well, my goodness, then," he said. "Imagine that. You've made me the happiest fellow on the planet!" He hugged her fiercely, but when he released her he saw that a shadow had passed over her face. "What's wrong?" he asked. "Are you having second thoughts already?"

"No, no. Not at all," she assured him. "I would be most honored to be your bride. But I'm afraid there are certain conditions."

"Conditions?" Marvin asked, trying not to panic, thinking he should've expected such a thing. He would deal with it, whatever it was.

"Conditions, yes. It's part of marrying a princess. I'm sorry about that. It's just the way things are. You marry a princess, there are always a few unavoidable preliminaries."

"All right, then," Marvin said, his delighted smile returning. "I can deal with that. Whatever needs to be done needs to be done, and I'll be happy to do it. You want me to get a blood test or take etiquette lessons? Consider it done." (It was this kind of reaction to situations, you see, that earned him the nickname "Marvin the Numbskull.")

"I'm glad to hear you say that, Marvin, because I love you very much."

He beamed and said, "I love you too, Oswalda."

"Now," she explained, "before we can be married, you need to prove your worth, not only to me but to my father, the king."

"Him too, huh?" Marvin asked, nodding at the face scowling down at him from the mantel.

"Yep."

As had happened so many times in the past, Marvin had allowed his enthusiasm to overpower his reason—this time actually knocking his reason cold and hiding it under some shrubs.

"You must perform three impossible tasks," she told him. Her expression now was one of utmost seriousness. "First, you must destroy Ogg Vorbis, the evil and vicious troll who lives along the banks of the Gowanus Canal, returning his bloody, severed head to me as proof. Then you must journey to the land where the moon sleeps and steal his blanket."

"The moon has a blanket?"

"It's a very nice blanket."

"I see . . . um, and why do you want a troll's head? Is it very nice too?"

The princess sighed. "No, Marvin. It's *not* nice. It's hideous. But I have my reasons, okay? Reasons that shouldn't concern you."

"But if we're to be—"

"Finally," she said, cutting him off in a clear dismissal of his concerns and an assertion of her princessly superiority, "you must travel back in time and prevent the assassination of Richard Nixon."

"But," Marvin broke in again, "Nixon was never assassinated."

"Then I guess that means you'll have to make two trips, doesn't it?"

They were silent for a moment. Then she added, "If you prove yourself worthy by successfully completing these three tasks, I will willingly and happily consent to be your loving bride. Should you fail—and if you're still alive after failing—my father will arrange to have your head removed from between your shoulders."

"Where's he gonna put it instead?" Marvin asked, the panic creeping into his voice. Then he stopped and his face grew calm again. He smirked and rolled his eyes. "Whoa, ho, ho," he said, holding up his hands, grinning with relief. "I get it. You almost got me there. I mean—what—you're kidding, right? That's it. The whole princess thing. It's a setup, right? Am I on TV?" He began looking around for the cameras.

"I'm afraid princesses don't kid," she informed him. "It's not in our nature."

"But we were joking around not ten, fifteen minutes ago."

"That was different. I wasn't in princess mode then. Marriage proposals require princess mode."

"Oh. I see."

Marvin pondered the situation, but for a surprisingly short period of time. He balanced the ridiculous and impossible tasks laid out before him with the beautiful and absurdly rich princess who was holding his hand.

"All right, then," he agreed. "I'll do it."

(What was that nickname again?)

Figuring it was best to get a jump on things, Marvin set off early the next morning for the subway that would take him across the river to Brooklyn. Over his shoulder was slung a bag containing a box cutter, a baseball bat, and a small pouch of red powder the man at the twenty-four-hour botanica assured him would weaken any troll long enough to lop its head off without too much fuss. Marvin knew next to nothing about trolls—hell, he wasn't even aware one was living right over there along the Gowanus—but he figured the things he carried with him would be more than enough to complete the task. It was the other two tasks he was more worried about.

He stepped off the train shortly after ten a.m. and began the short journey to the banks of the Gowanus. That a monster lived down there among all the industrial chemical runoff didn't surprise him. If there were trolls living anyplace in town, that would certainly be the place to find them. Or one of the places, anyway.

As he wandered past the houses he kept visions of Oswalda in his mind's eye, in order that he might focus on just why, exactly, he was doing this. His courage wavered for just an instant as he passed Sammy Joe's Casket Company but soon returned as he neared the canal. There was so much for him to gain.

The foul stench grew worse the closer he drew. Marvin wasn't sure whether it came from the canal itself (which was an unhealthy and opaque green) or from Ogg Vorbis the troll. He pulled the baseball bat from the bag and rested it against his shoulder, just to be on the ready.

When he finally reached the Gowanus, he scoured it up and down from where he stood, looking for any obvious signs of troll activity. He wasn't at all sure what troll footprints looked like but figured he'd recognize them when he saw them.

He lowered himself down to the banks of the canal, trying at all costs to keep his feet from touching the water. He once heard it could eat right through the sturdiest of shoes in a matter of seconds.

Once again he kept walking. From what little he'd read about trolls, he remembered they had a thing for bridges. He poked under the small metal bridge at Union Street and, finding nothing there, set his sights on the expressway in the distance.

"That's a much better bet," Marvin thought. "It's much less likely he'd ever be seen under an expressway."

As his steps brought him closer to the bridge he began noticing some unpleasant signs. Along with the old tires and broken computers, bones that appeared to be human began to litter his path. It was unclear whether they were the bones of Ogg Vorbis's victims or the bones of unlucky saps who'd gotten too close to the toxic and stinky canal.

Just to be safe, he reached into the bag again, pulled out the packet of anti-troll powder, and stuck it in his shirt pocket, where it might easily be reached in an instant.

Suddenly there was a great and terrible roar, which shook the earth and the very air around him. Marvin looked up quickly to make sure it wasn't just a tractor trailer rumbling down the expressway (which, of course, it wasn't).

Before he could register fully what he was seeing, the green water began to bubble and boil and a mighty beast arose from the unspeakable depths of the Gowanus.

Ogg Vorbis was easily taller than three men standing atop each other's shoulders. Short men, perhaps, but three of them certainly. His features were mostly hidden behind a thick mask of matted and burned black hair—all but his red eyes, which were as big as dinner plates (nice ones), and his sharp teeth, which erupted from his mouth every which way. His monstrous, shaggy arms ended in wicked claws and a necklace of human skulls hung around his neck. Gnarled crabs and rats and enormous blood-engorged leeches clung to his chest and legs, and his ragged shorts were much too small to conceal his mighty three-pronged penis.

"*Ho-lee shit!*" Marvin exclaimed.

The troll raised his arms and growled at Marvin in his frightful, hissing voice. "*Why are you bothering me, puny man with your punier stick?*" Then he paused and lowered his arms.

"No, wait. Let me rephrase that," the troll said. He cleared his throat gruffly. In a much calmer voice, he asked: "Why does that *bitch* Oswalda keep sending *losers* out here? . . . I mean, what does she see in creeps like you, anyway?" He squinted at Marvin with contempt. "No matter, I guess." He raised his arms and began with the hissing again. "*I will gnaw your eyes out and rip your arms from your torso, same as all the others . . . And you can't even begin to imagine what I'm gonna do to your ass!"*

In fact Marvin could imagine quite clearly what the troll had in mind.

Two hours later Princess Oswalda, who was lounging around her Chelsea apartment, sipping prune juice and listening to Burl Ives records, heard a loud knock on her door.

She set down her glass and opened the door, only to find her would-be fiancé standing in the hallway. His clothes were torn and soaked. He smelled really, really bad. His face was bruised and a four-inch gash on his left cheek was still bleeding. She looked at his hands and noticed he didn't seem to be carrying a severed troll's head. She looked at his face again and found him glaring at her.

"Well?" she asked.

Marvin continued to glare. Then finally he opened his mouth.

"*Fuck* this," he said.

He turned on his heel and headed back toward the elevator under the mistaken impression that no one would ever call him a numbskull again.

The Gnome Who Would Be King

Once there was a gnome named Gerard and he was pissed. He was shorter than everyone else, his skin was a sickly pale green, he had a long, crooked nose and pointed ears, and you don't even want to hear about his wardrobe. Worse, even within the gnome community, he was considered kind of a jackass.

The ironic thing about that last bit was that Gerard considered himself a tireless crusader for gnome rights.

After months of petitioning, he was finally granted an audience with the mayor in order to discuss some of his grievances.

He arrived at the mayor's office a few minutes early, took a seat, and accepted a cup of coffee from the secretary, who tried very hard not to stare at him. Then he had another cup of coffee. An hour later, after four cups of coffee, the secretary at last told him he could go in.

"About fuckin' time," he snarled at her as he climbed down off his chair and stomped past her through the office door.

These Children Who Come at You with Knives

"Why hello there, gnome," said the mayor, who was seated behind an enormous polished oak desk. "How can I help you today?"

Gerard climbed, huffing, into the chair opposite the mayor, then stood on the seat so he could look him in the eye.

"Well, Mayor, it's like this," he began. "We gnomes are grossly underrepresented in city government. On television too. We find it hard to get jobs, and when we can get jobs we're paid far less than our human counterparts doing the same work. About twelve cents to the dollar, in most cases."

"I see," the mayor said, wondering now why he had agreed to meet with the ugly little man, especially after so many of his letters had been laced with threats and obscenities. "And how would you like me to help you and the other trolls?"

"*Gnomes!*" Gerard snapped. "We're *gnomes*, all right? Can't you even get that fucking straight? You see? That's the problem right there! I come in to discuss the problems facing gnomes in a serious manner and straight off you start calling us trolls. You aren't even listening."

The mayor remained patient, for that was required of a man in his position. "I beg your forgiveness. I guess while I was talking, my eyes drifted over to this cute little troll doll on my desk." He held up the wide-eyed, pug-nosed plastic figure with the wild rainbow-colored hair. "See? A simple slip of the tongue, for which I apologize."

"Say, that's something. Could I see that a moment?" he asked, sticking out a stubby arm.

"Why certainly," the mayor said, handing it to him. "One of my daughters gave that to me for—"

Gerard hurled the troll doll across the room. "*There.* Now let's get down to business. We're sick and tired of only being able to find work in people's gardens. Do you have any idea how demeaning that is? 'Oh, come work in our garden! That would be so *cuuute!*' Then they always laugh, the assholes. We're sick and tired of it. We want government jobs. And business subsidies. And big tax breaks. Reparations, grants, whatever you got we want it."

The mayor considered this, then said, as patient as ever, "I'm sorry, Mr., uh, Gnome, but in this economy, we simply can't afford to go giving money to every group that asks for it. In our eyes, you're just like any other citizen. Shorter maybe, and with pointy ears, but apart from that—and the wardrobe—you face the same risks and get the same breaks as anyone else. Because of that, you'll have to make a go of it on your own, just like everyone else."

The green of Gerard's face darkened as he banged a tiny fist on the mayor's desk. "I am an ugly, deformed little gnome! You *owe* me! I want money! And power!"

"Mr. Gnome, please," said the mayor, trying to calm him down. "Yelling won't accomplish anything."

"It won't, eh?" Gerard sneered. "Then maybe this will." He dropped his sackcloth breeches and, glad now that he'd had that fourth cup of coffee, pissed all over the mayor's polished desktop.

Moments later, as two giggling security guards dragged the gnome from the office while a third mopped up the desk, Gerard screamed, "You'll pay for this injustice, Mayor! In the days to come, you and everyone like you in this stinking city— all you people who've been keeping us down for so long—will come to regret it! You will feel our wrath! You will be on your *knees* before me!"

"So he could look you in the eye?" one of the security guards snorted, moments before Gerard bit him on the thigh.

Word of Gerard's meeting with the mayor spread quickly through the gnome community. Most just shook their heads. Being peaceful and gentle creatures by nature, they all agreed that they wanted nothing to do with Gerard's crazy antics, and most were admittedly embarrassed that he'd come to be their public representative. Most, to be honest, were perfectly happy working in the gardens. It was far preferable to working in an office where everything would be out of scale and sterile, and they'd be forced to wear ties and shoes. They weren't interested in tax breaks and subsidies. They were quite content living and working under the radar and being paid under the table.

When Gerard began making the rounds of the public gardens in an attempt to scare up recruits for his social revolution, he found that he was almost universally ignored. None of his fellow gnomes wanted to hear about it. As he spoke, they continued tilling the rich soil and watering the daisies.

This infuriated Gerard even further.

"You dumbasses don't want to fight for yourselves? For your rights under the law? For what we all deserve as citizens? *Fine,* then," he chided. "You pathetic little cretins. But hear me. Even though you don't deserve it, I'm going to go out there and take care of things myself. Hear that? *Myself!* And one day all you filthy little dirt jockeys will thank me. Until then, fuck all y'all."

Then, as he set off on his quest for gnome rights, he cast a bitter glance over his shoulder at the mildly amused gnomes still toiling away and yelled, "Losers!"

Gerard's tiny legs carried him toward the center of town, and as he walked he tried to come up with a plan. For all his talking and yelling and attempted recruiting of an unholy gnome army, he still had no idea what he intended to do in order to achieve his goals. He'd kind of expected that the mayor would just give him what he wanted and that would be that. The fact that he did not complicated things.

The more he walked and thought and schemed, though, the more contempt he began to feel for those other gnomes who so willingly accepted their own servitude.

"Fuck them," he thought. "They don't want any more than that? They don't want my help? Then screw 'em. I'll take it all for myself."

Fact is, although he may not have been consciously aware of it—not that he'd admit, anyway—this idea had been at the back of his mind from the start.

The following day after reaching the center of the city, Gerard paused outside a diner on a crowded street. Out in front, two men were smoking and talking. One was bald and fat, the other was a tall, skinny man with sideburns.

Being hungry after such a long journey, Gerard decided to get a bite to eat in the diner. The two men, however, were blocking the doorway.

"Excuse me, my ugly oppressors," he said, "but do you think you'd mind moving your goddamn fat asses so I can go inside?"

Both men stopped talking and looked down at him.

"Hey look at that," the fat one said. "It's a foul-mouthed dwarf."

"That's *gnome*, you bloated fuck," Gerard corrected, glaring up at him with narrowed black eyes. "Get it straight. And get the hell out of my way."

"Gnomes are funny," the tall man with the sideburns said to his friend, ignoring Gerard. "They always want to sit up front." Both men laughed at this.

Gerard couldn't help but notice that as they continued talking they weren't moving. He took a step backward, his face twisting in near uncontrollable fury. It was a face so horrid that pigeons on the sidewalk next to him took flight. Then he began to waggle his stumpy fingers in the air in the general direction of the two men.

Now, unbeknownst to Gerard, there was something about the face—something about the configuration of contracted muscles and wrinkled green skin, the squinting black eyes and bared, misshapen teeth—that unleashed a dark and long buried part of the human psyche. That hate-gnarled face of his exposed something bad and humiliating, some thankfully forgotten memory people just wanted to leave behind. The effect his face had on people wasn't magical so much as it was primitive—a kind of primal psychological trigger that neither the victims nor Gerard understood.

"Christ, look," the fat man said. "I think he's performing some kind of wizardry on us!"

Then the fat man was a boy again, in the attic. His thin right ankle was chained to a pipe. It was hot and he'd burned himself. He heard the heavy boots on the steps, saw the enormous shadow, and knew what was going to happen. It had happened so many times before.

For years the man with the sideburns had told himself that he'd done the only right and decent thing when he unplugged his only child's respirator that night when no one was around. But now he saw her in the hospital bed again, her little arms flailing, her eyes pleading. He dropped the cord and reached for the pillow.

Both men teetered, grabbing at their heads as if to hold their skulls together. Then they turned and fled screaming blindly into the street.

The tall man with the sideburns ran headlong into a speeding livery cab and was hurled twenty feet in the air, while the fat man, amazingly enough, avoided all the traffic and made it to the opposite sidewalk, only to trip over a stroller and smash through the huge plate-glass window of a hardware store, where he was impaled across a display of awls, screwdrivers, and pinking shears. There was blood everywhere.

Gerard was delighted by this, and now that the path was clear he strolled into the diner, took a seat, and had a bowl of soup, ignoring the chaos in the street behind him.

"That was some trick," he thought as he ate. "These human assholes are so stupid and superstitious that I should be able to frighten them into giving me whatever I want."

That evening, he practiced a few more times, in order to ensure that the reaction of the men outside the diner wasn't a fluke. He jumped out of alleyways and from behind bushes, screwing up his face in the same way, yelling, *"Boo!,"* and wiggling his fingers at passersby.

Gerard couldn't have been more wickedly pleased with the results. They all screamed and ran, clutching their heads. Some even gave him their wallets and jewelry before doing so.

That night he took a room in a small hotel in a seedy part of town (where they were apparently used to dealing with creatures much stranger than Gerard), and he prepared for bed feeling quite satisfied with himself.

In the next morning's newspapers, however, there was only a tiny mention, written in an overly smug tone, about several pedestrians who told the police they had been accosted by "a tiny creature," "a monstrous little man," or "an evil dwarf." One of the victims told the police that "it was just like 'Three Billy Goats Gruff' or something."

Some victims reported seizures, migraines, nosebleeds, and broken toes in the aftermath.

Gerard crumpled the paper in his small hands and dumped it in the trash. He clearly needed to refine his technique. He wasn't just after people's wallets and jewelry (though he wasn't complaining about that). He wanted *power*. And before he was given power, he had to convince these stupid humans that he was for real and meant business.

The way to do that, Gerard concluded, was to choose his victims more carefully. He needed to find someone they couldn't doubt. Someone credible. Someone who was well respected.

What's more, he had to do something other than just yell "boo."

That night, he crept through the shadows and the alleys until he found his way to the opera house.

"Lots of rich and important assholes come here," he thought to himself, "even though they *hate* opera. The jerkoffs pay all this money to come here to be bored and see something they hate because they think they're supposed to." It was the perfect place to find a rube who would spread the word.

He hid behind a pillar outside the entrance and waited for intermission.

When the gray-haired men in tuxedos and their obese dowager wives in the finest of evening gowns began to filter outside to smoke, he scanned their faces, looking for someone he recognized.

His tiny black heart leaped when he saw Mr. and Mrs. Affenbottom separate from the crowd and move in his direction. Mr. Affenbottom, the CEO of an international banking conglomerate, was one of the wealthiest men in the city. At the moment, he and Mrs. Affenbottom were seeking a bit of privacy so they could continue the bitter argument they'd started in their town house several hours earlier.

"Just shut your ugly trap, Beatrice," Mr. Affenbottom was saying when Gerard sprang at them from the shadows, his dark eyes glittering.

"Make me your king!" he shouted, startling both of them.

"What the—?" Mr. Affenbottom blurted.

"Make me your king if you value your lives!"

"Oh, Robert, *do* something, won't you? Be a man for once," his wife said.

"Shut it, Beatrice," he snapped at her before turning his attention once again to the gnome, whose face was screwed up in a frightful display of crooked teeth and flared nostrils.

"Make me your king or I'll place a curse upon you!" He began again with the fingers.

"Oh, not another one," Mr. Affenbottom thought reflexively. He was quite baffled by all this. "Make you . . . what, now?"

"*Enough!*" Gerard shouted at the wealthy couple. "You can't harm me! I'm a gnome! A gnome, I say!"

"But I'm not trying—" Mr. Affenbottom began.

"If you don't grant me what I demand immediately," Gerard hissed at them, "I will curse you! A bad one too! On both you and your ugly-ass wife."

"Why I—!" she said indignantly.

"I'm still not real . . . umm . . . a king?"

"Your delay and your stammery ways have cost you dearly," Gerard sneered. Then he launched into the curse he'd written up that afternoon.

> *Up the winding mountain*
> *Down the rushing glen*
> *You dare not go a-hunting*
> *For fear of little men!*

It wasn't a real curse, of course, and Gerard was well aware of that. It was just something he'd heard in the movies once. It was for show, is all. As every magical and semimagical creature knew, curses are ninety-nine percent psychological. All that mattered was that they sounded good enough to make the victim believe. And Gerard thought this one sounded pretty damn good. Combined with his contorted face, he couldn't lose.

Mrs. Affenbottom began sobbing (less out of fear than at having been called ugly assed), but something happened inside Mr. Affenbottom's head. An old memory exploded across his consciousness.

He was eight years old, and three of his friends had grabbed him one summer afternoon, tied him up, and laid him across the railroad tracks on the south side of town, all the while telling him that the train was coming. Little Bobby screamed for his mommy and wept for mercy. Then, as all three boys began laughing hysterically, he wet his pants.

The memory began to play out a second time, and a third, and as it did Mr. Affenbottom realized in horror that his tuxedo pants were suddenly warm and damp.

He turned away from Gerard, slamming into his sobbing wife before the two of them fled as fast as wealthy people are capable of fleeing.

The following night, Gerard placed the same curse on a professional baseball player, the night after that on the deputy mayor, and the night after that on the fire commissioner. They all ran screaming and slapping at their skulls as if to knock the thoughts out, convinced even as they ran that their limbs were withering and their fortunes souring as a result of the encounter.

By the end of the week the headlines of the local newspapers—even the respectable ones—screamed, "City Terrorized by Magic Gnome!"

That tickled Gerard, but as he read them he couldn't help but notice that something very important was missing. None of the stories mentioned anything at all about his being made king.

Most of the stories instead concentrated on how unpleasant it must be for the rich and famous to have to encounter the ugly and poor.

Worst of all were the artists' renderings. One police sketch left him looking like Gabby Hayes, and another, in one of the tabloids, simply reproduced a drawing of Grumpy from *Snow White and the Seven Dwarfs*.

"Oh, he isn't even *trying!*" Gerard said, as he once again crumpled the papers in his small hands.

Despite his general displeasure with the coverage, it was now clear his actions were having the desired effect.

The mayor, who had long since forgotten his own encounter with Gerard, was forced to hold a press conference in an attempt to calm the jittery public.

"It's probably just kids playing a stupid prank," he announced. "Little hooligans who ought to be horsewhipped. And when they're caught," he added, "I'll pull down their pants and do that horsewhipping personally!"

The mayor's creepy promise of corporal punishment satisfied few. As fear of Gerard spread, the city ground to a halt. The fire commissioner had locked himself in his office, where he drank gin and wept while morale dwindled among the ranks. Soon several neighborhoods were ablaze, but no one in the fire department could muster the courage to go fight the fires, out of fear they might encounter the wicked gnome. In solidarity, the police soon followed suit, spending their shifts huddled together in station houses instead of fighting crime.

The baseball player, superstitious to begin with as most sports figures are, misunderstood Gerard's words completely in his hysteria and convinced his fellow teammates that, if any of them ever stepped on a baseball field again, their arms would fall off. With nobody playing baseball, no fans were compelled to go out to the stadium.

Shop owners left their stores shuttered, and the Dow Jones industrial average plummeted. Residents were afraid to leave their houses at night. The deputy mayor shot himself, but only after shooting half of the city's councilmen. Soon thereafter, those members who weren't shot resigned.

Society as a whole began to crumble. Hundreds died in the fires the firemen refused to fight. Hundreds more died during the wave of assaults, rapes, and murders that followed the desertion of the police force. The streets were littered with the bloating and dismembered corpses of innocent short people who'd been mistaken for the gnome and were ripped limb from limb by blood-crazed mobs.

As Gerard thumbed his way through the newspapers in the days that followed, he couldn't have been more delighted, artists' renderings aside.

"Burn, baby, burn!" he chuckled maniacally. Even though it wasn't being reported, surely his demands must have reached the top levels of government by now. They would have no choice but to make him king!

Not wanting to appear too eager, however, he decided he would wait until they contacted him and begged him to take over.

After three days had come and gone and no one had contacted him with an offer, Gerard began to grow bored and antsy. Perhaps cursing a few more prominent figures would speed things up.

Since he hadn't tossed his curse at anyone in a long time, he thought it might be best if he had a practice run, just to make sure he still had his chops down. So that evening he headed out once more through the alleys and the shadows until he spied Mickey the Town Retard sitting on a steam grate.

"Aha!" Gerard thought. "This will be so simple it's not even funny. This moron'll be so shocked by the sight of me, he might just up and croak!"

As he crept closer to Mickey the Retard, he began to notice the stench. Gerard also noticed the empty bottles of vodka and Clamato juice, as well as the cowbell. Mickey's clothes were filthy and tattered and he wore a moth-eaten orange stocking cap. He was unshaven and his fingernails were black with grime. On his lap was an old gray mail sack, which contained all of his earthly possessions.

"It's almost a shame," Gerard thought, "to waste my talents on an imbecile like this. But what the hell?"

He leaped in front of the man and made that horrid face of his. "Boo!" he said. "Make me your king!"

Mickey stared at him with world-weary but slightly amused eyes for a moment before asking in a slow and controlled voice, "What . . . in the *fuck* . . . do you think you're doing?"

"I'm . . . I'm scaring you," said Gerard, caught off guard.

Mickey shook his head. He might've been retarded but he was no dummy. "No you're not. You're annoying me. There's a difference. I'm just sitting here thinking, minding my own business, and some little gnome jumps out and starts yelling at me. What the hell's *that* all about?"

"I want to be your king," Gerard explained, now feeling a bit embarrassed.

"Now why," Mickey asked, "would you want a damn fool thing like that? From the looks of you, my guess is that people hate you enough as it is—especially if you keep annoying them the way you're annoying me. You become king, they'd only hate you three times as much. Maybe four."

"But . . . I want power."

"Oh, power schmower," Mickey snorted. "Sounds like a bad case of attempted overcompensation if you ask me."

Gerard, realizing that this wasn't going nearly as well as he'd expected, decided to jump straight to the big closing number.

"Enough of your insolence!" he barked. "For that, I'll place a curse on you!" He waggled his fingers at the retard's face and intoned:

> *Up the winding mountain*
> *Down the rushing glen*
> *You dare not go a-hunting*
> *For fear of little men!*

When he was finished he let his arms fall limply to his sides. Mickey the Retard not only seemed less than terrified—he seemed utterly unimpressed.

After a moment's silence to make sure the gnome was quite finished, Mickey asked, "What do you take me for, some kind of retard? I've seen *Don't Look in the Basement*. And it wasn't scary then either . . . Unless you're actually trying to quote William Allingham, in which case you're getting it wrong. What the hell does that even mean? 'You dare not go a-hunting'? I've never been hunting in my life, and I don't plan to start now. And you're a little man and I'm not afraid of you. And, Christ, what the hell's a *glen*?"

Gerard was at a loss.

The thing with Mickey was this: Gerard's face was powerless against him. See, being a retard (even a really smart one), Mickey had never experienced personal humiliation or shame. Nothing he perceived as such, anyway. Gerard's visage might just as well be triggering memories about changing his socks or finding a stick.

Then the idiot sighed. "Look," he said. "I sit here on this grate because I don't want to be bothered. I like it that way. Just me and my vodka, my Clamato juice, my cowbell, and my own thoughts. I'm perfectly happy. So tell me—if I give you something nice, will you go away and let me be?"

He opened the sack on his lap and emptied the contents on the sidewalk next to him. Out of the sack spilled three filthy socks, a comb, a mason jar filled with a thick black liquid, a feather, and three dented aluminum cans.

The mason jar caught Gerard's eye. That might be useful, he thought. But as he was bending over to examine it more closely, Mickey the Retard plucked him up by the nape of the neck, dropped him in the empty (and smelly) sack, and closed it tight.

Then he stood, flung the sack over his shoulder, and, with Gerard kicking and screaming all the way, trudged across town to the bridge that spanned the widest and deepest river in the region.

Halfway across the bridge Mickey stopped. Then he swung the bag once, twice, three times above his head before casting it, with the gnome still inside, to the cold and dark waters below.

Being a professional retard, he was unfamiliar with the various behavioral tics and phobias common to all gnomes. He wasn't aware, for instance, that gnomes in general were deathly afraid of water and, as a result, never bothered learning how to swim. He was just trying to get the little fucker as far away from him as possible.

As the story goes, Gerard kicked and flailed and gurgled in fear, but the bag sank like a rock to the very bottom of the river, where the gnome presumably drowned and, over time, was eaten by small fish.

News of the wicked gnome's demise spread and soon the fires were put out, the baseball players began to play ball again, local government chose a few new members, and shop owners reopened their stores. And Mickey the Town Retard was hailed as the greatest hero the ruined and smoldering city had ever known.

At the ceremony in which he was presented with a golden medal for ridding the city of that scourge of a gnome Mickey the Retard spoke to the adoring masses.

"I'm not a hero," he announced from the podium. Everyone applauded his humble modesty and sang his praises. Then he raised his hands for silence. "No," he said, "I'm not a hero. I'm a retard. The only reason I'm here is because *you* people are all a buncha stupid babies too damn scared of your own shadows and too willing to believe ridiculous stories." Then he left the stage without another word. Everyone cheered him as he went.

Later that night he pawned the medal and used the cash to buy himself some more Clamato, several bottles of top shelf vodka, and a new canvas bag. A bigger one this time, because you never can tell what sorts of things you might come across. Then he returned to his steam grate and sat down. He was happy to be back.

Just to be on the safe side and prevent anything like this from ever happening again, the mayor arranged to have all the remaining gnomes in the city—gentle, peace-loving, and reasonable creatures that they were—rounded up and imprisoned. Then, without benefit of a trial and with the best interests of the city in mind, they were publicly hanged, five at a time.

Plants Ain't No Good

Not too long ago, in a town not unlike your own, a man named Nick Bogus returned home from his job on the night shift at the shoe factory. More specifically, this particular factory supplied a chain store called Really Big Shoes, which sold oversized footwear to oversized ladies. It wasn't bad work, he figured, so long as he could keep his mind off the fact that he was a mere cog in the construction of cheap and uncomfortable fake leather footwear for fat chicks.

Nick ran the press that punched the eyelets in each shoe that came down the line. This meant that over the course of every eight-hour shift he pushed a button several thousand times, and that was about it. It didn't pay very much, but without him pushing that button nobody would be able to properly lace their shoes.

His wife, Euglina, didn't bring much in from her job at the mop store either. Between the two of them, however, they got by comfortably enough. Their needs were fairly simple, and they had no interest in kids, which kept their expenses even lower.

It was shortly after six a.m. when Nick finally pulled the keys from his left pocket to unlock the door of their third-floor apartment. He opened it just a crack and stuck his head inside.

"Euglina?" he whispered. "You awake?" She usually wasn't at this hour, but you never could tell with her. Sometimes she surprised him. Not often, but sometimes. This time, as usual, there was no response.

Nick opened the door the rest of the way and, quietly as possible, tiptoed over to a chair so he could take his shoes off. But feeling around in the darkness, he sensed that something was amiss. The chair was always in the same spot in the corner, but it sure as heck wasn't there now. He turned his body and continued sweeping his arms in increasingly wide arcs, waiting for them to bump something. Apart from the wall and the closet door all he felt was still air.

"Hmpf," he thought. "She must've rearranged the furniture without telling me." He reached over for the standing lamp to shine a little light on the situation, only to find that the standing lamp had been moved too.

"I'll be," he thought. "She's sure been busy." It seemed odd that Euglina would go about rearranging furniture when she was so mortified by the very idea of housework in general, but who knows? People get ideas sometimes.

Nick was well aware that turning on the overhead light would likely wake her up, even though the bedroom was down a short hallway and the door was probably closed. Euglina was sensitive about light and sound that way. Even if she didn't see the light, she'd be able to hear the filament buzzing, and she wouldn't be happy about it. But she'd have to understand, he rationalized, that not knowing where anything was he might well trip and break his neck in the darkness, and heaven knows she wouldn't want him doing that.

He flicked the switch, winced briefly against the brightness, and looked around the kitchen for the chair. She'd moved the furniture around, all right. She'd moved the chair and the lamp . . . and the table . . . and the coat rack, and the pictures on the walls, and all the little doodads and ceramic figurines she'd so lovingly arranged on the shelf. She'd moved everything—every scrap of everything in the front room, in fact. The room was completely bare.

He walked into the small living room, thinking she'd moved everything in there, maybe so she could wax the floor (and the walls), but that room was empty too, right down to the floorboards.

Nick found this all very peculiar. Best thing to do, he thought, was to go wake up Euglina and find out what the deal was.

As he walked down the hall, he couldn't help but notice that everything appeared to be gone. *Everything.* The apartment seemed completely barren, and his footsteps, in a way he never noticed before, echoed off the clean white walls around him. He did have to admit, in spite of it all, that the place seemed a little bigger for it.

When he reached the bedroom door he found that it was open.

"Euglina?" he asked again, still keeping his voice down.

And though it shouldn't have surprised him by this point, he was nevertheless quite surprised to find that the bedroom was also completely empty. The bed, the dresser, the throw rugs, the framed photos, and the nightstand were nowhere to be seen.

He wasn't fretful or worried yet—just very, very confused. None of this made any sense to him. He wished Euglina would step out of the bathroom or something and give him a simple and rational explanation. Had they been robbed by a team of extremely thorough burglars? Had she decided to renovate the place on her own? Had repo men shown up? Had some sort of heavy-duty extermination job been arranged without his knowledge? He'd never noticed any serious roach problem.

The big question, though, was where in God's name was Euglina?

Nick stood there helpless, staring at the empty bedroom.

Empty, that is, except for the sheet of paper he finally noticed lying in the middle of the floor.

He bent and picked it up. The handwriting was definitely Euglina's, and he breathed a sigh of relief. The note, he thought, would provide the simple explanation he was looking for. And in a way it did.

Dear Idiot, it began.

You're such a fucking idiot. Do you know how big of an idiot you are? Obviously not, so I'll tell you . . .

The note went on to describe (in unnecessarily graphic detail, Nick felt), the yearlong affair his beloved wife Euglina had been having with some guy named Osgood she'd met on the

Internet. Osgood, she claimed, was "five times the man" Nick would ever be.

It went on for a while, the note, and variations of the word *idiot* were used extensively. Nick still had no choice but to read every word. The gist of it was that she'd met this Osgood character in a chat room, quickly began a torrid affair, and had decided to run away to the Scottish Highlands with him. Not only with *him*, as it turns out, but with everything Nick and Euglina owned as well.

She'd taken the furniture, the television, the stereo, all the pots and pans and plates, the records, the flatware, the books, and the telephone. She even took his clothes, which, in an astonishing twist, fit Osgood to a tee.

"Must've used a pretty big U-Haul," he thought absently as he read.

Down at the very bottom of the note, underneath where she'd written "Drop Dead!" and signed her name, there was a small postscript.

By the way, I did leave the plant behind, because I know how much you love it.

She was being sarcastic, of course. Euglina herself may have loved it, but the plant—or, as Nick tended to think of it, the Plant—was the one thing in the world he truly and deeply hated.

He hated the Plant to the very core of his soul. More than mosquitoes, more than his boss, more than people with cell phones, Nick despised the Plant. He wasn't even sure why he hated the Plant as much as he did. Maybe it was because he always felt a little jealous of the way Euglina doted over it, watering it, trimming its branches, adding nutrients to its soil. She could sometimes spend hours every day tending to the damned Plant, which was a lot more than she ever offered Nick. She even *talked* to the Plant more than she talked to him.

Given how much she loved it, he found it strange that she would choose to leave it behind while taking all of his ELO records. But he guessed, as the note seemed to imply, it was just another way of kicking him in the gut.

"Well, shit," he said aloud, as he crumpled the note and let it fall back to the floor.

He was still quite numb, the full ramifications of what had happened having not quite hit him yet. He had nothing left—no clothes, no bed, no phone, no cooking utensils. He didn't even want to think about what he'd learn when he went to the bank later to check on their joint account. All he had left was that loathsome Plant.

He wandered through the empty apartment, in and out of each of the small rooms, checking in closets and in corners to see if there was anything at all she might have missed—a sock, a scrap of soap, some mustard. Anything he could hold on to. There wasn't.

Except for the Plant, which he found hanging in its usual spot near the front window.

It really was a hideous thing, a small evergreen bush whose branches stuck out every which way without any apparent rhyme or reason, like sickly green spiny tentacles. She had it hanging from the ceiling in that same spot since they'd first moved into the apartment a decade earlier, positioned in such a way that he couldn't even look out the window without noticing it and shuddering with revulsion.

Seeing it now, his first impulse was to throw open the window, grab the beastly flora, and send it crashing to the sidewalk below. And in fact this is what he fully intended to do. But after taking three steps toward it, his rage turned to sorrow, as his wife's betrayal, thievery, and cheap insults pierced his heart fully for the first time.

Nick collapsed in a heap to the floor, curled up on his side, grabbed his knees, and began sobbing.

"Oh, *why, why why?*" he wailed, as the tears flowed from his eyes and pooled on the floor beneath his cheek.

A guy named *Osgood* yet!

"How could she have done this to me?" he whimpered, lightly banging his head against the wooden floorboards.

He rocked and moaned and wept long into the afternoon, until at last he heard a someone say, "Good God, would you *shut up?*"

Nick's wailings stopped abruptly and he sat upright. Still sniffling, he asked, "Who said that? Euglina?"

With hope in his heart, his eyes darted about the room, fully expecting to see Euglina standing there, about to explain that it was all a joke, and that he was on one of those cruel prank shows.

"Christ," the voice said, "you're such a sap."

It sure sounded like something Euglina would say, but she was nowhere to be seen.

"Euglina?" he asked again, slowly getting to his feet.

"It ain't Euglina," the voice said. "She's long gone with that new sucker of hers and she ain't coming back."

Nick's immeasurable sorrow now shifted to fear and confusion. "Then . . . then who said that? Who's talking?"

The voice sounded exasperated this time. "Oh, lemme give you three guesses, jackass."

Nick's attentions finally turned to the only other living thing in the room.

"But," he said, his voice filled with bewilderment, "you're a *plant*. Plants can't talk."

The Plant emitted an audible sigh. "Fine then. So I guess I'm not a plant."

"But . . . if you aren't a plant . . . then what are you?"

The Plant sighed again. "Your soon to be ex-wife was right. You really *are* a fucking idiot, aren't you?"

"So . . . ," Nick asked, his voice hesitant, "you read the note?"

"Note?" the Plant replied. "I didn't read no note. But I have been listening to her prattle on and on all these years. Every day the same goddamn thing—what a fucking idiot that Nick is. Every time that Osgood creep was here, too, they'd talk about almost nothing except what a big stupid jerk you are."

Nick said nothing, not really in much of a mood right then to hear more about what his wife really thought of him.

"But if you ask me," the Plant said, "if they wanted to see a couple of morons, they shoulda looked in the mirror. What kind of parents name their kid *Osgood*, anyway?"

"A real *jerk*," Nick suggested.

"Damn straight," the Plant agreed.

"This was more like it," Nick thought.

"Jesus," the Plant went on, "I've never heard two more tedious, insipid, unimaginative cretins in all my life. Yap on for hours and say nothing at all."

"Yeah?" Nick's spirits were at last beginning to lift.

"Listen," the Plant said. "You ask me, you're better off without her. She was a skank, and a fool at that. You deserve better. Lord knows I'm glad the bitch is gone. There were times, swear to God, that if I were capable of strangling her I would have. Just to get her to shut the fuck up."

Nick seated himself down on the floor once again, and over the course of the next several hours he and the Plant regaled each other with stories about what a lousy piece of trash that Euglina was, and how they were both mighty glad to finally have her out of the picture. Even if she did take everything Nick owned.

"Look here," the Plant said. "You I always kind of liked. You know why?"

"No," Nick said, suddenly feeling quite ashamed for having harbored such a profound animosity toward the Plant for all these years.

"Because you minded your own damn business, that's why. You did your own thing and let me do mine. You weren't always over here poking and prodding and trimming and yakking. Like she had anything to say. She was such a fucking pest. And *shrill*? God, that voice of hers could scratch steel."

"Boy, could it, huh?" Nick said, recognizing for the first time what an incredibly annoying voice his presumably former wife had. Especially when she tried to talk in that "baby doll" voice she thought was so cute. It wasn't cute. It grated on his nerves and made him want to retch—though he'd never told her that, or even admitted it to himself until now.

It didn't take long for Nick to be all turned around on the Plant issue. This Plant was a-okay in his book. It might have been hideous to look at, but he was well aware that he was no prize himself. Besides, anyone who hated Euglina as much as he was coming to hate her sure couldn't be all bad.

And considering his circumstances, the Plant was the only thing he had left. That would be much easier to accept if he could get along with it.

Over the next several weeks Nick Bogus began to build his life anew. He continued going to his job at the shoe factory as usual, used his paychecks to open a new bank account, and slowly began to replace the things his wife had taken, starting with a small stereo and some ELO records.

He bought a new and much larger pot for the Plant and placed it on the floor to give it more room to grow. The Plant was quite grateful for this.

"You cannot believe how cramped I was in there," it told Nick. "My roots were all knotted up and sore. They were choking in there."

Nick never told anyone that he was living with a talking plant. Not that he wasn't tempted. After all, who the hell else has ever heard of a talking plant? But he didn't dare share his secret, as very early on the Plant had warned him against it.

"Look," it said one evening, as they were discussing the viability of various get rich quick schemes. "I gotta warn you straight off here never to tell anyone that I can talk, okay? No one at all. Don't even *hint* at it, no matter how tempting it might be. If you're at the factory and someone says, 'Hey, wouldn't it be something if plants could talk?,' don't go saying, 'Hey, I got me a talking plant at home!'"

"Why not?" Nick asked. He had to admit he'd considered the possibility of taking the Plant on the talk show circuit or something. They could probably make a quick bundle together.

"First of all, you shouldn't because I'm asking you nicely not to. And second, even if you do spill the beans, no one would believe you. Either they'd think you were schizo and hearing voices and they'd lock you away or they'd think you were pulling some kind of cheap ventriloquist stunt. Either way, it would never fly. And I'll promise you right now that if you ever bring anyone else back here, you won't get a peep out of me, even if you talk to me directly. Hell, even if the *house* caught fire I wouldn't say squat."

"Any reason why?" Nick asked.

"*Because.* How's that? It's just my way, and I'll thank you not to push me on it. Remember, for all those years she was gabbing away at me, I never spoke a word to that douche bag, because I didn't feel like it."

Realizing he should respect the Plant's wishes, Nick promised he wouldn't breathe a word of his plant's gift, and he never did.

*   *   *

As time went on, the Plant thrived. It grew and grew, its branches spreading out wider and taller. If it was in need of water or a trimming or an even larger pot, all it had to do was tell Nick, and Nick would take care of it. And if Nick got the sense the Plant wasn't in a talking mood, he wouldn't push it. They got along just fine that way.

Meanwhile, as the Plant grew and grew and grew, its branches soon all but covered the front window. Nick offered to trim them back a bit but the Plant always refused.

"Nah," it would explain. "I'm doing this for you, Nick. Just my way of saying thanks for not throwing me out the window that day Euglina split. I know you were tempted, and I guess I wouldn't have blamed you."

"Oh, I would never have done that for real," Nick said. "I was just pissed at her at the time."

"I know that, but still, this is for your benefit. She took the blinds, after all. And I know it can get awful bright and fiercely hot in here, especially with the summer coming. Not only will my branches help keep the place cool and shady, they'll also keep any nosy fucking neighbors from peeping right in here. You deserve a little privacy, don't you think?"

Nick, clearly touched by the gesture, thanked the Plant sincerely and never again asked if it wanted to be trimmed back. If it did, he was sure it would tell him.

But slowly and quietly—so slowly and so quietly in fact that Nick never would have noticed even if he'd been looking for it—as the Plant grew over the windows and closer to the ceiling, it was also growing in other ways as well. Its roots began to snake their way out of the tiny holes at the bottom of its pot and, hidden from Nick's view, inched their way over to the wall. They burrowed into the floor and into the space behind the drywall, mingling with the electrical wiring, the plumbing, and the telephone lines.

From there, the roots climbed both up toward the roof and down toward the sidewalk and the building's foundation.

Although neither Nick nor anyone else could tell from looking, over the course of a year the Plant had essentially become one with the house, feeding directly from both the plumbing and the electrical systems—having a perpetually replenished water supply was a tremendous convenience as well as a luxury.

With an endless water supply coursing through its xylem and electricity—real electricity instead of some sugar solution crap—flowing through its phloem like some fantastic drug, the Plant felt a power it had never known before. Its limbs grew at an unprecedented rate, soon pressing against the ceiling above it and the walls to either side. Even more astonishing, the Plant had also discovered that, with a little practice, it could even move its branches at will, no longer having to depend upon that useless and unpredictable sunlight.

It also found that tapping into the phone lines was, if nothing more, a good source of entertainment during the long, slow hours while Nick was away at work. The Plant not only picked up on new bits of language it had never heard before but was able to keep up with the news and learn the embarrassing naughty secrets of the other people who lived in the building. (The guy in 2C, for instance, had a real thing for latex.)

Nick may not have been aware of the various wanderings of the Plant's root system, but there was no ignoring this recent growth spurt, which he put down to the homemade mulch he'd recently been mixing with the dirt.

"Wow," he said one afternoon, shortly before heading out for the shoe factory, "look at you, huh?"

"It's something, ain't it?" the Plant replied, flexing a few of the branches it knew were blocked from Nick's view.

"Sure is. Like that mulch, huh?"

"Mulch?" the Plant snapped, then caught itself. "Oh yeah, yeah, the mulch. It's really great, *Mmm-mmmm!*"

"I'm certainly glad to hear that. I wasn't sure if you'd like it or not."

"Oh, yes, yes. You bet. Superb mulch, if I do say so. Come on, sit down here near me. Let's talk."

"It would be a pleasure," Nick said, taking a seat and glancing at his watch. "I need to head out for work soon, but I always have time for a chat."

As the Plant began talking, however, Nick noticed something. It was talking much faster than usual, its words at times colliding into one another, and not always making the clearest sense. It was much louder than usual too.

It wasn't just the way the Plant was talking that caught Nick's attention—it was what it was saying. Suddenly it was using slang terms Nick wasn't familiar with, along with words such as "ginormous," "yo yo yo," "pimp daddy," and "dude." It was even sharing gossip about the other tenants of the building, most of whom Nick had never met. He had no idea how the Plant could've known some of the things it did, but he didn't think that much of it or anything else, putting it down to that new mulch.

The time he would normally leave for work came and passed as the two continued with a wide-ranging conversation that was more animated than usual. A conversation that edged Nick closer to deciding it really was time he told someone about this talking plant of his. It was something much too remarkable to keep to himself. Plus, if he could make a few extra bucks on the side because if it, what's the harm in that? Maybe he could finally get away from that stupid shoe factory.

Hours passed, and despite the energetic and fascinating discussion (especially when it came to gossip about the neighbors) Nick found himself growing sleepy.

"Sleepy?" the Plant asked. "Then by all means take a nap. You can lie down right there on the couch if you like."

"Yeah," Nick said groggily, "I may just do that. Wake me up in half an hour or so, will you?"

"Sure thing," the Plant assured him.

Nick moved over to the couch and lay flat on his back, his hands folded on his chest, and soon he was snoring loudly.

The Plant waited, patient and still, until it was absolutely certain that Nick was sleeping like a baby. Once he was, the Plant openly flexed a few limbs. It felt mighty good.

Over the course of the next eight months, the Plant grew and grew and grew some more, bursting from the constraints of its pot, its branches filling the room completely, pressing against the ceiling and spreading out toward the kitchen. Its root system, meanwhile, burrowed its inexorable way into the solid foundations of the building, then back up into the walls again, seeking nourishment and entertainment.

One spring afternoon, a nine-year-old girl named Jolene Winkley was in the process of tormenting her cat, Booger, with a chopstick. Booger had just hissed again and taken another swing at her when Jolene noticed a crack in the floor of her family's basement apartment. As she watched, the crack grew longer and wider. Unbeknownst to her small and undeveloped mind, this was not a good thing.

Similar, parallel cracks were appearing in all the apartments directly above Jolene's.

Then, much to everyone's surprise, with a great rumble and groan and *kkrrrricch*, the entire building split in two, spilling bricks and dust and furniture in a great tumble toward the sidewalk.

In the days that followed, rescue workers, firemen, and insurance adjusters pawed through the rubble, looking for survivors and answers.

Booger was found unharmed, but Jolene was a goner, that's for damn sure, squashed the way she was beneath the family's collapsed grand piano.

"Guess you'd call that *A Flat Minor*, huh?" one of the firemen asked with a grin after coming across the smear of child beneath the remains of the Steinway.

The one thing that had them all scratching their heads was the gigantic plant in what had been the third-floor apartment.

Hundreds upon hundreds of branches coiled and poked every which way, at times growing so thick that workers needed to send out for machetes in order to cut through the foliage. Nobody had a clue as to how a simple houseplant could've grown to such enormous size in a small apartment like that. It defied all explanation. And where was the owner? Who'd been taking care of it?

It was only then, after chopping their way through a particularly thick knot of branches, that they found the mummified body of Nick Bogus, who was still stretched out comfortably on the couch.

Misery & Co.

There was once a very sad and impoverished man who lived in a shabby apartment in a desolate section of Queens. Grady was his name, and it had been quite a long time since anything had gone right for him. Eight months earlier, he'd been fired from his job at the pencil factory. It wasn't a great job, but it had paid the bills and kept food on the table. He hadn't been able to find any work since.

Fed up with his lack of initiative, his wife had packed her bags, grabbed the kids, and moved to Jersey, leaving him all alone. And now the landlord was threatening to have him evicted for being three months behind on his rent.

His clothes grew threadbare and smelly, as he could neither afford new ones nor even spare the quarters necessary to do a few loads of laundry. For food, he'd taken to hanging out near the dumpsters behind area grocery stores, waiting for nightfall so he could rummage through the discarded bruised vegetables and dented cans.

His days grew slower and heavier, and he wandered the streets of the city, stopping at each business he came across to ask for work. He was often sent away before he could finish asking on account of his foul smell and unkempt appearance. Sometimes he was granted an interview, but usually only as a cruel joke. It was never very long before he found himself back on the sidewalk, his face as long as a rainy week.

Soon, the dark cloud of despair that for some time had been nothing more than a figure of speech became a reality, gathering a foot or two over his head, following him wherever he went.

Many was the time a small child walking with his mother would point and ask, "Mom, what's that all about?"

"Shhh, dear," the mother would reply. "Don't point. It's just a nimbus."

"What's a nimbus?"

"Well, honey, a nimbus is a dark cloud of despair, and if you get too close you could end up with one too."

Things got only worse for Grady. Some of the food from the grocery store dumpster left him with an intestinal infection, and the mold that grew up the walls of his apartment left him wheezing and coughing up gobs of black phlegm laced with blood.

One day, Grady raised his eyes to the heavens, intending to implore God to tell him why he was facing such troubles. Instead of heaven, however, he found himself staring into his dark cloud of despair. And staring back at him from the cloud were two dirty yellow eyes.

"Hello, Joe, whaddya know?" asked a shrill and grating voice from behind the yellow eyes.

As we can all imagine, this filled Grady with some astonishment. At a loss to say anything else, he replied simply, "My . . . my name's Grady, not Joe."

The yellow eyes squinted at him, and the cloud began to dissipate, leaving a yellow-eyed monkey floating where the cloud had once been.

"I know that, dumbass," the monkey said. "It's just vernacular."

"I see," Grady said, still staring up at the floating monkey. "Um . . . who are you?"

The monkey smirked (as much as such a thing is possible) and said, "That's always the trickiest of questions, ain't it? Let's just say I'm here to help you."

"Help me?" No one had ever offered to help Grady in any way before, so the prospect made him very happy.

"*Sure* I'm here to help you. I've been following you around in this cloud here for a while now—I'm guessing you noticed."

"I thought it was just a metaphor."

The monkey shook his head. "Nope. It was me. And I've been watching how you go about things, trying to figure out how best to turn your life around."

They agreed to return to Grady's apartment so they could discuss matters more privately, and so Grady didn't have to stand there on the sidewalk, craning his neck.

The two of them walked back to Grady's place, so perhaps now would be a good time to explain that the monkey hadn't been exactly one hundred percent completely straightforward with him. If Grady had asked, in fact, he might have learned that the monkey's name was Misery, and he was, officially, a

Homunculus of Despair. He'd been around long before the cloud appeared, and it was his job to ensure that things would go as badly as possible for poor Grady.

Grady didn't know that, though. He was so thrilled at the prospect of receiving some help that it never occurred to him to distrust the monkey.

"Now," the monkey said later, as the two of them sat in Grady's meager kitchen, "the way I see it, your primary problem—at least the most important problem facing you right now—is money. Am I right?"

"That's a pretty big one, I'd say, yeah."

"Of course. If you got some money, you'd be able to pay your back rent, buy some real food, and, *Christ*, wash your damn clothes. Then we'll go on from there."

"That's sounds like a good plan," Grady agreed.

"Of course it is," the monkey chastised. "I'm a magical creature. What the hell did you expect? Now, as the old chestnut goes, it takes money to make money, right?"

Grady sighed. "That's the problem, I guess. What do you want me to do, sell off all my stocks and bonds?"

The monkey sneered. "Don't be a wiseass, okay? I'm here to help you."

"Sorry. I guess I can't help being a little cynical."

The monkey ignored him and continued. "What we're going to do is start small. If we can raise just a few bucks, you could clean yourself up and get something halfway decent to eat. If you're more presentable and feeling better, it'll make everything that follows that much easier. So now," he said, letting his eyes drift around the apartment, "what do you have here that you can sell?"

The poor man and his new magical monkey friend went through every inch of the apartment. There wasn't much to be found, but there were a few things that could probably bring in a couple bucks. He had a small television set and a radio. He even had a portable stereo that was still in mostly working order, and some records to go with it.

"I'm not sure I want to part with this Roy Orbison box set," Grady said. "That's really set the mood for me these past few months."

"Then that's part of the problem," the monkey said. "Attitude." He snatched the box from Grady and tossed it near the other things they had gathered together. "If you still want it once you're back on your feet, you can buy a new copy."

Next, they pulled the blanket off Grady's creaky bed and carried everything outside. After spreading out the blanket on the sidewalk, they set the television, the stereo, and everything else in as handsome and presentable a manner as possible.

"Now," the monkey said, "I'm going to hide in the dark cloud again, if you don't mind. Can't afford to have anyone seeing me."

"Sure," Grady told him. "I think I can take it from here."

By the end of the afternoon, much to Grady's delight, almost everything on the blanket had sold, and he had nearly fifty dollars in his pocket.

After Grady had carried the blanket back inside, the monkey reappeared. "Great work out there, Grady. Now you can afford some laundry, a few decent meals. Hey, you can even buy some new clothes with that kind of scratch!"

The two danced around the apartment for a bit until, with an enigmatic smile, the monkey stopped. "You know what?" he asked. "This calls for a celebration. This was just a small first step, but you're on your way. I think we should go get a drink."

Grady, caught up in the moment and under the impression that his troubles were at an end, agreed.

The monkey disappeared into his cloud again and the two of them went to the nearest bar, where Grady, urged on by the monkey, bought round after round— one for himself and one for the monkey who, being magical, was able to drink without being seen.

Before he knew it, Grady had spent all of his money. And not having had a drink in so very long he was also quite snockered.

The thing about Grady—which he himself had forgotten but that Misery the monkey knew quite well—was that he was an awful, cantankerous drunk. After one drink or ten, he would get loud and boastful and belligerent, poking his finger into the chest of whoever happened to be nearest him.

Grady woke up in the gutter several hours later, with his teeth chipped, his ribs sore, and his nose caked in dried blood.

Through bleary, blackened eyes, he saw the monkey grinning down at him.

"Whoa, bad news there, pal," the monkey said. "Those guys really did a tango on your face."

The monkey helped him to his feet and walked him home, where Grady flopped onto the bed and immediately fell into a dreamless, drunken sleep.

He awoke late the next morning still battered and aching and with the worst hangover he'd ever had in his life.

The monkey sat next to him clucking his tongue as Grady puked again and again into the filthy toilet.

"Okay," the monkey said, "so you kind of blew all your money last night. But like I said, I'm here to help. That was a minor glitch, and now we just need to start all over again. We can do that." Then, although Grady couldn't see it, the monkey's eyes narrowed deviously. "But before we get started again we need to take care of that hangover. Would you like that?"

Grady nodded weakly and rasped, "Yeah."

"Well then, there's no better way to take care of a hangover than with a little hair of the dog."

Once again, albeit more slowly this time, they went through the apartment, collecting things that might be sold. Most all of the good stuff had been sold the day before, so today they moved on to second-tier crap. Pots and pans, old magazines, coffee cups.

Once again, they dragged the blanket outside. The items they laid out didn't bring in nearly as much as the things sold the previous day, but it was still enough to afford a few drinks to clear up that hangover. Once that was taken care of, they could get down to the real work of turning Grady's miserable life around.

Although he had only three or four drinks at the bar, once again he let his tongue get the better of him, and upon the monkey's urgings he decided not to take any shit from anybody.

The next morning Grady felt awful again, and though he

couldn't remember anything that had transpired at the bar, he was worried that his jaw, three of his fingers, and at least one rib might be broken.

Again, the monkey shook his head. "All right," he said, "getting the program under way is taking a bit longer than I planned. I think the lesson here is that you shouldn't have any more than a couple drinks at a time. Then you gotta stop."

Grady merely nodded.

"But to get those couple of drinks, we still have to sell a few things."

This time Grady was forced to sell his sheets, his lamps, and the photo albums that contained all the treasured pictures of his wife, his kids, and the happy life he once led.

This cycle, if you can imagine, rolled on for several weeks before Grady, so desperate to believe anything, noticed that his life had grown much more awful since the monkey first made his presence known.

"Look," he finally told the monkey one night, "things haven't gotten any better since you started helping me. In fact, they've grown much, much worse. I feel like shit all the time. I've been banned from bars, had trouble with the police, and was nearly killed at least five times that I can think of."

"Seven," the monkey corrected. "But you were pretty out of it, so I guess you didn't notice."

"I don't have any money and I've nothing more to sell."

It was true. A glance around the apartment revealed that he had sold everything. All the furniture, the rugs, the lights, even some of the plumbing fixtures.

The monkey looked contrite as the two of them sat there on the floor. "I know," he said, his yellow eyes downcast. "Things haven't gone exactly according to plan. But tell you what. I'm going to make it up to you."

"Yeah?" Grady asked doubtfully. "When? Six months after I start selling my ass over on Tenth Avenue?"

"That won't be necessary," the monkey assured him. "And to be honest, I don't know if it would be all that profitable anyway. No, I mean tonight. Right now." He stood up and walked to the door. "Come with me."

Grady still had his doubts, but he followed the monkey outside. What choice did he have?

The pair walked for many hours, as Grady allowed the monkey (hiding in his dark cloud) to lead him.

At last, after finding themselves in a part of Brooklyn Grady had never visited before, the cloud came to a stop at the entrance to a dark alley.

Grady looked around. "What are you stopping here for? This doesn't look too good."

"In there," the monkey commanded, one of his thin hairy arms appearing from the cloud and pointing toward the alley.

Grady peered into the dark alley, shook his head, and took a step backward. "Uh-uh," he said. "No way. Go in there and get stabbed or shot? Hell with that."

"There's no one in there," the monkey assured him. "We're all alone."

Grady, still uncertain, asked, "And what am I supposed to do once I'm in there?"

"I'll show you. Trust me. It'll be worth your while."

Not believing him for an instant, but not knowing what else to do, Grady followed the cloud into the darkness.

After his eyes adjusted, Grady saw it was just an ordinary, filthy alleyway, with garbage, broken bottles, used needles, and puddles of urine. Five battered trash cans were lined against one of the walls. At least it was as empty as the monkey had promised.

"Now," the monkey instructed, "go take a look in the last garbage can down there."

Walking carefully and taking regular glances over his shoulder, Grady approached the fifth garbage can and, fully expecting to find a thug with a knife hiding inside, slowly lifted the lid. All he found was an expensive-looking black leather bag.

"Open the damn thing," the monkey hissed.

Still expecting the worst, Grady pulled the bag from the trash can. It was much heavier than he'd expected. He set it on the ground, flipped the latches, and opened it.

Stuffed inside were bundles upon bundles of cash—twenties and fifties mostly, it seemed. He quickly slammed the case shut again as his body began to tingle.

"There," the monkey said. "Don't say I never did anything for you."

"But . . . ," Grady asked, his eyes wide with fear. "Whose is it?"

"Whose is it?" the monkey replied. "It was in the trash, dummy. It's *nobody's*. It's *yours*."

The two of them carried the heavy bag back to Grady's apartment as casually as possible, with Grady trying unsuccessfully to control his sweaty face and shaking hands.

"What is it?" he whispered to the monkey when he was certain no one was within earshot.

"It's *cash,* idiot," the monkey replied. "Moolah, greenbacks, the cold hard."

"But—but how did you know about it?"

The monkey sighed in mild exasperation. "I'm *magic,* remember?"

Grady, perfectly willing to accept that, didn't bother to ask why the monkey hadn't done something like this much sooner.

Once back at his apartment, they shook the bundles of cash from the bag onto the bare and dusty floor and began counting.

An hour later, after two recounts, they found that the bag had contained one hundred and fifty-seven thousand dollars, give or take.

"And it's all yours," the monkey said proudly.

Grady was beside himself. "We must celebrate," he said. "But we don't want to go flashing this around at a bar. They'd get suspicious." Then he smiled. "I know. We'll be very frugal tonight. Yes, we'll have a frugal celebration. Then sleep on the money and tomorrow start making some real plans, all right?"

"That sounds good," the monkey said, no longer concerned about how long it would take. His work, in fact, was all but finished. Grady would do a perfectly fine job of destroying himself from this point on.

Taking a single twenty-dollar bill from one of the bundles,

the two went to the grocery store and bought the makings of a nice but simple dinner.

On the way home, Grady suggested they stop in to an Italian specialty shop called Lumpy's. "Just one extravagance," he told the monkey. "This place sells the best olives I've ever had. I'd love to get a big bucketful."

"Be my guest," the monkey replied, and they went inside, where Grady bought a three-gallon container of black olives.

"Really like olives, huh?" the guy behind the counter asked as he handed over the enormous Tupperware container.

"I sure do," Grady told him with a broad smile.

After unpacking the groceries back at the apartment, Grady opened the bucket of olives and said, "I'm going to wash these off in the sink first."

After dumping all the olives out of the bucket, he set the container next to the sink and called the monkey over. "Could you do me a favor? Could you take some pieces of bread and mop up all the excess olive oil at the bottom of this thing?"

"Oh," the monkey said. "Sure thing." He tore a hunk of bread from the loaf they'd just bought and set to mopping up the oil. But small as he was, and big as the bucket was, he found that he had to climb all the way into the three-gallon container to get to the oil at the very bottom.

The moment the monkey was in the bucket Grady, quick as a flash, slapped the lid back on the container, burped it, and threw the now trapped monkey demon into the black leather satchel that once held the cash. Then he closed the bag and ran out the door.

"Hey!" the monkey shouted from his new cage. "You don't know what you're doing!"

Grady, who had grown a bit more clever over these past few weeks, knew exactly what he was doing. He knew the monkey was trouble and, if allowed to stick around, he would surely destroy everything. He was misery incarnate, Grady thought, unaware that this was in fact the monkey's true name. One thing he did know was that since the monkey was able to turn himself into a cloud, no normal container could hold him. Hence the three-gallon Tupperware bucket. That was the only thing that might work. (In reality, Grady hated olives.)

He took the bag and the protesting monkey to a distant park where, feeling a burst of adrenaline, he flipped over a large rock. He dug a deep hole, dropped the bag into it, then rolled the rock back atop it.

Brushing off his hands with satisfaction, Grady felt much lighter—giddier even. He returned home, had a nice dinner, counted his money one more time, then threw the olives away.

Contrary to what Misery the monkey assumed, Grady did not squander the money, nor throw it all away on booze.

He paid off his back rent, acquired a new wardrobe, which was far from extravagant but still very nice, and made wise and careful investments. He even had the mold cleaned out of his apartment, and received the training he needed to get a decent job as a podiatrist's assistant. Last but not least, he not only replaced his Roy Orbison box set—he bought himself a Bob Wills box set to boot. Although he soon used up all of the money he had found in the garbage can, he'd spent it so wisely that he was soon completely back on his feet again. He wasn't making millions at his job, but he was making more than he had made at the pencil factory, and it was plenty to keep him comfortable. He no longer had to go dumpster diving or lay curled in his bed praying that whatever illness he'd contracted would simply go away on its own.

Things were going so well, in fact, that he even contacted his wife, explaining the recent turn of events and asking if maybe she and the kids would like to come back so they could live together as a family again.

She had no interest in that at all, as it turned out, but that was okay. Grady knew that, should he ever feel like it, he could easily meet another fine woman.

As things stood, Grady was as happy and as satisfied as he could ever remember being in his entire life. He'd learned his lesson with that monkey and vowed to be wise and careful in his future decisions.

Well over a year later, as he was enjoying his favorite medical drama on the television and thinking again that someone really should come up with a medical drama featuring podiatrists, Grady heard a knock on his door.

This was odd, as he wasn't expecting anyone. He pushed himself up from the sofa and opened the door. There he saw four very large, very well dressed men.

"Good evening, sir," one of the men said with a smile. "Is your name Grady, by chance?" He was a distinguished-looking gentleman, with a healthy tan, dark eyes, and black hair that had gone gray at the temples.

"Why, yes—yes it is," Grady said, very surprised by all this.

"Ah, good," the man said, still smiling. "I must say, it took a very long time to find you."

"Find me?"

"Yes, but now that we have, everything's going to be just fine."

"Oh," Grady said. "That's good."

"Good for us, certainly," the man said. "I believe you have something of mine, and I would like it back, please."

"I'm sorry?" Grady asked, genuinely confused.

"I'd like my money, please."

Something went cold in Grady's intestines. "Your . . . money?"

The distinguished-looking man breathed through his nose. Then he patiently explained. "You found a bag in a trash can. A bag full of money. *My* money. I was on my way to retrieve it from the alley that very evening but you got to it first."

Grady began to sweat. "I'm afraid I really don't know what this is all about."

A gleeful, grating voice chimed in: *"Hello, Joe, whaddya know!"* moments before Misery the monkey popped his grinning head above the distinguished-looking man's broad shoulder.

The man continued speaking as if he was utterly unaware of the monkey on his shoulder. "May we come in please and talk things over?"

Grady, so confounded by everything, merely took a step back and let them enter.

"Thanks for the ride, boss," the monkey said as they passed, before leaping onto Grady's shoulder.

The four men took seats around Grady's small living room as Grady whispered furiously at the monkey. "I got rid of you! Can't you take a hint? You bury someone under a rock, it generally means you don't want them around."

The monkey just smiled at him.

"Why can't you go live with this guy?" Grady asked, nodding toward the man who was calmly flipping through the television stations while waiting for Grady to be finished with his insane muttering. "Why can't you make *his* life a living hell?"

"No can do, there, chum," the monkey offered, shaking his head. "I'm *your* misery. And each man's misery is his own. You got no choice in the matter, and to be honest neither do I. I couldn't go away with him if I wanted. Which is too bad, because his house is really sweet."

"Oh," was all Grady could manage.

"And it seems I have a lot of lost time to make up for." Misery then disappeared into his dark cloud again.

Lost and hopeless, Grady turned back to his unexpected guests.

"So let's lay things out plain and simple, Mr. Grady. You found a large quantity of money that did not belong to you. You brought it home with you, which is understandable, as you're only human. But you're also a citizen. You didn't take out ads, you didn't put up flyers, you made no effort whatso-ever to find the money's true and proper owner, as you are expected by law to do. If no one shows up after two weeks, then you may legally keep it. But only if you make some effort to find them first."

"But no one asked—"

"Of course no one asked, you peabrain, because you didn't *advertise*. Had you advertised, we would've been able to retrieve the money a long time ago, and we wouldn't be having this pleasant chat now."

"I'm sorry," Grady offered, ignoring the wicked cackling cloud over his head.

"Let me explain," the man continued, much too calmly, Grady thought. "Not having that particular money at that particular time caused me a great deal of trouble. Business trouble and otherwise. People got hurt. My reputation was damaged. But all of that is in the past. All I ask is that you return the money now, and all will be forgotten."

The three men who accompanied him were eyeing Grady in a way that made him less than comfortable. He wondered whether he should offer them some sort of refreshment. But he couldn't move.

"So where is it?"

"*Refreshments?*" Grady squeaked out.

"The money."

"I—I don't have it anymore," he said in a thin voice, as the tears welled up in his eyes. He knew he was a dead man.

In a jumble of tangled phrases and confused time frames, he tried to explain all that had happened, from losing his job, through his time with the monkey, to pulling himself back together, thanks to the money that wasn't his.

When he was finished there was a cold silence in the room.

"That was very heartwarming," the man eventually said. "Except for the part about the invisible monkey. That didn't make much sense at all."

"Sorry."

"But I take it that what you're trying to say in the end is that not only don't you have my money on hand, you don't even have it in a form in which it could be obtained in cash, am I right?"

Grady nodded.

"You spent it on food and cheap clothes and learning a trade in order to make a meager living."

Grady nodded again.

The man smiled. "That's all quite admirable. I would've been much more upset if you'd spent it on jewelry and fancy cars." Then he paused. "Then again, jewelry and fancy cars we can take from you. But we can't take an education. And we really don't want those clothes."

There was more silence. It felt to Grady like his intestinal infection was returning.

"All right, boys," the man said at last, placing his hands on his knees. "Let's go home."

Grady's body went limp with relief as he watched the large, well-dressed men stand.

He headed for the door to open it for them. "I'm so sorry about all this," he said. He was being earnest. "I wish I hadn't listened to that monkey. But if there's any other way—maybe at some point in the future—that I could make it up to you. Hey! I know— Do any of you suffer foot pain?"

The man stopped in the doorway and turned back to the three others, who were walking a safe distance behind him.

"No rush," he said to them, holding up a hand. Then he turned to Grady. "I've been looking for that money for a very long time, as I said. And there was much hardship involved. So now that it's clear you cannot return it to me, I'm afraid my own pain must be eased with yours, which you, too, will suffer for a very long time." Turning back to his accomplices he said only, "Take it slow, boys. Especially you, Noodles. Make it last."

Then he turned and left, closing the door behind him, leaving Grady alone with the three hulking thugs and Misery the monkey.

Misery lived happily ever after.

Schotzie

Things were never that easy for Schotzie. Not by a long shot. Yet somehow, no matter how bad things became, it never got him down. You never once saw him dragging his knuckles, eyes downcast, a cloud of dismal gloom over his head.

No sir, Schotzie always had a big smile.

Schotzie wasn't his given name, of course. That came later. No, when he was born in the long-ago year of 1939 in the faraway town of Piscataway, New Jersey, Schotzie's parents had named him Miguel Biebels. His parents, Margaret and Rodney Biebels, weren't really sure why they'd chosen to name their son Miguel, but it had seemed appropriate at the time.

He was their first and only child, and they loved him very much. He was raised in a comfortable middle-class household, with indoor plumbing, a backyard, a driveway, and a connected garage. When he was old enough, his parents vowed, they would make sure little Miguel had a swing set to play on.

Strangers may have looked at him funny when he was taken out for walks or to the store, but no one who knew the Biebels ever brought up his appearance, not even while drunk. The Biebels seemed perfectly happy, and Miguel was obviously well cared for, so why rain on their parade?

Because of this, it took Rodney (a successful paint salesman) and Margaret (a manicurist in a neighborhood beauty parlor) a few years to finally come to accept the fact that Miguel was not only a sock monkey, but a *microcephalic* sock monkey to boot.

Once they did accept the hard truth, however (lord knows there was no getting past it), they began looking around for someone or something to blame. It couldn't have been *their* fault, could it? Neither smoked or drank much, Margaret had taken very good care of herself while she was pregnant, and there was no family history. Nothing that they were aware of, anyway. It had to be something else.

While lying in bed at night, they spoke in hushed, conspiratorial tones about "That Day at the Beach," "The Tongs Incident," and "That Thing with the Spare Tire," desperately hoping to find an excuse for Miguel's condition outside of their own flawed genetic makeup. In his frustration one night, Rodney even accused Margaret of having an affair with some sock monkey she'd met at work, but he quickly apologized for suspecting such a thing of his beloved wife.

As they struggled in vain for an answer, they couldn't escape the truth. Whatever the cause—accident, nature, or punishment from a cruel God for some unknown transgression—their son was a pinheaded sock monkey, albeit a very happy one.

Patient doctor after patient doctor explained to them that no, there simply wasn't any way to increase the size of Miguel's skull. And even if they could have done such a thing (perhaps with some space-age polymer of some kind), they still wouldn't be able to do anything about his brain, which was roughly the size of a Brazil nut. And even if they could make his brain grow somehow, there was *absolutely nothing at all* they could do to alter the sad fact that he was a sock monkey. Mostly they just shrugged and looked sympathetic. That's what he was, and that's what he would remain.

The Biebels even visited a few doctors who promised them miracle cures for poor little Miguel, but those "cures" mostly entailed taking the Biebelses' money and sneaking out of town in the wee hours of the morning.

By the time Miguel was twelve the medical bills (both legitimate and scammed) had simply become too much of a strain on the Biebelses' already meager income. Plus the day-to-day, almost hour-to-hour care their son required had forced both of them to cut back on the number of hours they worked each week. It was all becoming far too much for them to handle.

So they did the only true and honest and right thing a couple of parents in their situation could do—they took Miguel to a traveling carnival at the local fairgrounds and sold him to a sideshow impresario for twenty-five bucks and a newfangled coffeepot.

"Well," Rodney was heard to say after Miguel, carrying a tiny brown suitcase, had been loaded onto the train south, "'least a coffeepot don't need a slew o' doctors. Breaks down, ya just toss it."

"Oh, you," Margaret giggled, elbowing him lightly in the ribs as they waved good-bye to their son.

For Miguel, whose tiny brain seriously limited his capacity for fear, separation anxiety, and loneliness, it was a grand and exciting adventure. Then again for Miguel and his tiny brain, each and every day was a grand and exciting adventure.

Sammy Krapwell, a man known as much for his girth as for his showmanship, was the Sideshow King of the Mid-Atlantic States. At least that's what he liked to call himself, and no one was of a mind to tell him any different. He'd been in the business a long damn time now, and though most everyone thought he was scary and fat—and maybe even a bit of an asshole—there was no denying he put on one hell of a show. And Miguel—or "Schotzie," as he would now be known—was going to be his new star attraction.

Pinheads might have been a common sight on the sideshow circuit in those days, and there were a few shows that had a sock monkey act. But Sammy Krapwell, who had to keep tabs on such things in order to stay ahead in this business, knew for a fact that there were no performing pinheaded sock monkey acts out there. He'd just cornered that market.

Everyone connected with the show fell in love with Schotzie straight off. Even the nastiest and sleaziest of roustabouts liked him. How could they not? He was so open and good-natured. Best of all, he always had a big smile for everyone, no matter what the weather or living conditions were like.

Simply putting him up on stage for the gawkers wasn't

enough, and Krapwell knew that. So at first he tried to teach Schotzie a few simple tricks—spinning plates, bouncing balls, biting the heads off snakes—but none of those really worked out very well. Schotzie would lose interest and let the plates crash to the ground, or he'd cuddle with the snake, who appeared to love Schotzie in return.

Then he thought of pairing up Schotzie with Ermond, the Human Pincushion. It seemed a natural, the pinhead with a pincushion, but then he couldn't figure out anything the two of them could actually do together. Making things even worse was Schotzie's tendency to weep openly when Ermond did his act, convinced he was hurting himself. The only time he lost his smile was when Ermond began pounding those tenpenny nails up his own nostrils. Krapwell couldn't very well put a sobbing pinheaded sock monkey on the stage—that'd just be pathetic.

As Krapwell tried to figure out what to do with him, Schotzie would wander the midway before the gates opened every day, eating corn dogs and cotton candy, his heart filled with giddy awe at the lights and the music and the smells. He waved at all the other carnies, and they waved back at him. Sometimes the girls who worked the special shows in the back even kissed him on the cheek. This was the best place ever, he thought.

Then Krapwell hit upon it.

At the third stop that summer, a dusty burg called Egg Stomp Hollow (never the most lucrative stop on the tour), he tried a little experiment. He dressed Schotzie up real nice in a pristine white Nehru jacket and stood him at the ticket booth in front of the ten-in-one.

"I want you to sell tickets for me today, Schotzie," he said, not bothering to explain his motivations. "It's the most important job in the whole show, and I'm counting on you."

Schotzie clapped his paws excitedly. No one had ever entrusted him with such an important responsibility before, and he was determined to do a good job.

Well, the rubes loved Schotzie. They loved the little sprig of hair at the tippy top of his pointed head. They loved his close-set eyes. And most of all they loved the fact that he always had a big smile for them. They were much happier and more comfortable buying tickets from Schotzie than from some hopped-up, chain-smoking tattooed thug.

The only problem was that Schotzie, being a pinhead and thus a little slow, simply wasn't that sharp when it came to making change. Sometimes he gave too much, sometimes not enough.

Krapwell fully expected this, and therein lay the genius of his plan. He pulled Schotzie aside after the first three hours and double-counted the take so far that night. (To be honest, with the overs and the shorts, things pretty much balanced out.) Anyway, he told Schotzie to stop making change, period. If someone gave him a twenty-dollar bill for a one-dollar ticket, he was to give them the ticket and a big smile, but nothing else.

Schotzie smiled and nodded at Krapwell, then went back to his post and stopped making change.

When the suckers complained, Schotzie would smile again, and shrug, and point over at Krapwell, who was usually standing near the exit to gauge the faces of the blowoff crowd leaving the tent.

And when someone went over to complain to Krapwell, he would tell them, "Hey, you gave your money to the sock monkey? Go talk to the sock monkey."

If they then went back to Schotzie to demand their change, he would, of course, just smile again. There was no getting around it. Not wanting to be seen pummeling a gentle pinheaded sock monkey in public, most of the customers simply gave up after a few frustrating minutes and went into the show.

The sideshow's take doubled, not only at that stop but for the entire season as well. The following year it went up again. The year after that too. While traveling carnivals across the nation were struggling, Krapwell was riding high.

Schotzie continued selling tickets and everything was swell. In his own quiet way, he had become the star attraction Krapwell knew he'd be from the beginning.

Then, many long and happy years after acquiring Schotzie for twenty-five bucks and a coffeepot, Krapwell—who by this time had become a very wealthy man—died in a freak Ferris wheel accident. No one knew those things could roll that far.

Krapwell's passing left Schotzie alone in the world. When the boss died, no one had any desire to step up and run the show in his stead, and so it was disbanded, everyone going his or her own way. Ermond, the bearded lady, the Siamese twins, the roustabouts—everyone packed up and vanished. After all those years of taking care of Schotzie on the lot, no one involved in the show considered even for a moment the possibility of taking him along with them to make sure he'd be okay. One day he woke up and they were all gone. No one had even bothered to say good-bye.

Worse, Schotzie was being cast into the world almost penniless. For all of Krapwell's riches, and in spite of the fact that Schotzie had made those riches possible, his will (which ironically enough had been scribbled on the back of a flyer advertising some Egg Stomp Hollow dates) had left everything to some guy named Stan who'd bailed Krapwell out of a North Carolina jail back in 1943.

This didn't get Schotzie down, no sir. He packed a few belongings in his small brown suitcase and headed out on what would surely be a new grand and exciting adventure.

By this time television had all but killed off the traveling carnival industry. And even if it hadn't, the art of displaying living medical anomalies for profit had fallen from favor in the public eye. The freaks, it was decided, belonged in hospitals and institutions. They'd still be stared at, they just wouldn't get paid for it, is all. Any thoughts Schotzie might have had about signing on with another show were pretty much screwed from the start.

That was okay too.

First thing he tried to do was go back home. He hadn't seen his parents in many long years, and he was sure they'd be happy to see him again. His mom might even make him some lunch.

When he arrived in Piscataway, however, he learned that, after they had sold him, Rodney and Margaret changed their name, moved away, and were in all likelihood dead by now. So Schotzie continued walking, thinking he might run into them somewhere.

He didn't, but in the end he did okay for himself. He got by, riding the rails and making a go of it here and there, more or less, stopping strangers on the street and asking them, "Hey, you got two tens for a twenty?"

Last time anybody saw him was in July of 1982, stumbling unshaven and semicoherent around the annual Brat Fest in Sheboygan, Wisconsin. The Nehru jacket had lost a few buttons and was a little looser on his frame than it used to be, but it was still white as white can be. And Schotzie? Well, let's just say that he still had a big smile.

Tubercular Bells

*L*ike all obsessions, Milton Fernhull's began quietly. Milton was an assistant manager at an upscale housewares store who discovered the hard way that one of his neighbors had neglected (again) to pick up after his or her dog. It was the third time that week, and Milton had about had enough.

"I've about had enough of this crap," he told his wife. "And I'm going to find out who's responsible. The sidewalks around here are like minefields, and it's getting worse every day."

Since he usually stepped in dog poop in the mornings, he figured whoever the responsible party was must be walking the dog (or dogs, from the looks of it) at night. So that evening he set a chair in front of the window overlooking the street and waited.

For hours he waited and stared out the window before at last giving up and going to bed. Yet the next morning, sure enough, there was more dog poop than ever on the sidewalk. Beyond that, there were several splattered gobs of spit and a few splashes of vomit.

"This is insanity," he told his wife that night. "It's no way for people to live. If I'm going to catch this person, I'm going to have to stay up all night."

His patient wife put on a pot of coffee. Milton took his coat by the window and waited all night, his ears straining to catch the tiniest jingle of a dog collar or click of dog nails on the concrete, the sound of someone retching or spitting—anything at all that would signal his sidewalk was about to be sullied. Come sunrise, he had neither heard nor seen anything. Yet an hour later, as he left for work bleary eyed and fuzzy headed, he found himself standing ankle deep in the biggest pile of dog poop he had ever seen.

As if that wasn't bad enough, the entire sidewalk in both directions had become a river of bodily fluids. Snot and puke and pus and bile and piss all flowed together in a thick noxious stream dotted with islands of shit. Great clouds of fat blackflies hung low over the flood, and even in the chill autumn air the unimaginable stench made Milton's own gorge rise.

Confronted with such a nightmarish landscape, most men would have screamed or called the police or written a strong letter of complaint to the EPA. Not Milton, who had almost expected this.

He didn't simply want to identify the culprit anymore. He wanted revenge. This was a malicious premeditated attack aimed at him personally. He knew that. And whoever was responsible would pay.

That night, instead of waiting by the window, Milton stepped outside, crossed the street, and hid in a darkened, recessed doorway. From that vantage point he could see a good stretch of sidewalk in either direction. He would hide in that doorway as long as it took.

The streets were silent. Even the cars were asleep.

At the stroke of four, as Milton's eyelids began to grow quite heavy, he caught a quick movement across the street to his left. A shadow dashed beneath a streetlamp. He strained his eyes but could see nothing.

There was another dark flash to his right. In the pool of light he definitely saw a small leg.

Another figure came dancing around the corner, fully visible, and Milton nearly let loose with a yelp of surprise.

It was a tiny man, no more than three feet tall. He looked human, apart from the pointed ears, the stupid haircut, the peaked red cap, and a pair of strange curly-toed boots. Aside from the hat and the boots, the little man was naked as a jaybird.

Not just naked, Milton noted with revulsion, but pissing as well. Dancing in circles and pissing.

In his hands he held a crystal bucket. Milton couldn't tell what was contained in the bucket, but whatever it was the little man was splashing it on the sidewalk as he danced and pissed. The bucket, though tiny, seemed to hold a bottomless supply of something thick and green.

A second little man, equally naked apart from the hat and boots, came dancing down the block, snorting and spitting an endless stream of phlegm in every direction.

Soon there was a third and a fourth and a fifth. They appeared silently from every direction, and each one was expelling a different bodily fluid onto the sidewalk in front of Milton's house. One was bouncing along on his hands and knees, pausing every few yards to take an enormous dump. Others were doing things Milton didn't even want to contemplate.

After the past three days, it struck Milton that this was the only thing that made any sense at all. Elves.

"Well, I guess I have my answer," he thought.

The strangest thing of all about the fantastic scene before him was that these bodily fluid elves, or whatever the hell they were, were completely silent. The elaborate choreography of their movements seemed to suggest they were all dancing to the same tune, but it was a music Milton could not hear.

At that moment, quite abruptly and unexpectedly, Milton sneezed.

The elves froze in mid-prance and a dozen tiny heads turned to stare at him. Despite his fear Milton stepped out from the shadows to face them. He had come here to confront them and confront them he would.

In an instant the elves flitted across the street and surrounded him. They didn't look happy.

The pissing elf with the bottomless bucket of goo approached him first. Milton stood still, staring at the little naked man and wringing his hands.

"That was pretty close," the elf said in a cartoon chipmunk voice, "but not quite. It should be wetter. Think of it. Come morning, who would be disgusted or inconvenienced by a mere sneeze? You need to give them something that sticks, see? Something they'll remember. No, I'm afraid you'll have to do much better than that."

"I'm . . . ," Milton began, "I'm afraid you don't understand. I'm not auditioning. I came out here to find out who was making such a mess of my sidewalk. I wanted to ask you to stop. It's very bothersome."

The crapping elf smirked. "You think we don't know that? It's our *job*."

"But—why?"

"Why do we do it?" The pissing elf shrugged. "Why the hell not? We could give you all sorts of fanciful explanations about the good we're doing for humankind by pissing on your sidewalk, but it'd just be a bunch of horseshit. No pun intended. Fact is, we like it."

"And people bug us," another added. The others nodded their small heads in agreement. "Especially the people in this neighborhood."

"Look at this." The spitting elf took Milton's hand and led him over to a nearby SUV. "A Sierra Club bumper sticker on a machine like this? Does that make any sense? If it was meant to be a joke it'd be one thing. But it's not."

"I . . . take the subway," Milton protested weakly.

"Oh, that's *super*," said the crapping elf. "So you consider yourself environmentally aware?"

Milton sensed that he was being cornered. "Yeah, I guess so."

"Then what could be more natural than shit and piss and snot? They're all completely organic. Yet when they show up on your nice, clean cement sidewalk, whoa, watch out."

All the elves tittered.

The pissing elf held up his hand for silence, then stared at Milton. "You get the idea. You complain and obsess about who's dirtying your precious sidewalk, but we don't see you out here with a hose cleaning anything up. You just bitch and moan and wait for someone else to do it."

"I just think," Milton tried to explain, "that people should take responsibility for their own messes."

All the elves again laughed merrily at that.

"Oh, man, that's a good one," one of them said, wiping away a tear. "I gotta use that."

"But now that I know who you are and what you're doing—"

"What," the spitting elf snapped. "You're gonna call the cops and tell them that a bunch of elves are out here shitting on the sidewalk every night? You gonna tell your *wife* that you were out here chatting it up with a bunch of incontinent elves? That'll go over real well. Hey, maybe you could even post some flyers around to warn the neighbors."

Milton nodded sadly, resigned. What could he do? "Well then," he said, "could I ask a favor?"

The spitting elf shook his head. "Sorry, pal. We don't grant wishes or any of that crap. We just do what we do."

"Hold on a minute there, Jerry," the pissing elf said. "We might be able to do something to make this human's life a little easier. After all, he may be stupid, but he's behaved very well here tonight. Remember that lady in Detroit?"

"Oh, man, I'd forgotten about her."

"What . . . did you have in mind?" Milton asked.

"We're gonna make you one of us!" they all squeaked in unison.

"Oh, now," Milton said, taking a step backward, "I don't think I'd really . . . No, uh-uh. I have a job."

"Don't piss yourself, ducky. We're not going to make you an *elf*-elf. Just an honorary elf."

All the elves took two large steps backward. Before Milton could register or react in any way, the pissing elf was swinging the crystal bucket around and around above his head. "Ah one-ah anna two-ah," he said.

With a sharp underhanded swing, ten gallons of thick, green goop flew from the bucket and splashed in Milton's face, coating his glasses, smearing his hair, and dripping down the rest of him. His skin began to prickle and burn.

"Yaahh!" he shrieked, his hands flying to his face. The stench was unbearable. He slapped at his hair and his clothes and his cheeks long after the burning had stopped. Now it was just cold and slimy. He could hear the elves giggling at his antics.

"Yeah, that's real funny," he said. "Thanks." He removed his glasses and wiped the lenses on the only clean, dry section of his shirt, then replaced them.

"There," the pissing elf said. "Now you're one of us. In an honorary sense, at least. Gooble-gobble, as they say."

As Milton watched in drippy, stinky, slimy amazement, all the elves began to dissolve, until there was nothing there at all. Not even a mist or a twinkle. He was standing alone across the street from his apartment, his clothes soaked, his hair thick with slime.

Understandably confounded by the entire episode, Milton crossed the street and returned upstairs. By the time he reached his door his clothes were completely dry. His hair was a little stiff but otherwise fine. His glasses, oddly enough, were cleaner than they'd been in months. The stench was gone. He removed his clothes, went to bed, and slept soundly until it was time for work. Although it had been only two hours, when he awoke he awoke energized and refreshed.

At the stroke of four the next morning Milton was awakened by a wondrous music from outside. He'd never heard such lovely music before. It sounded like a thousand tiny bells in perfect harmony. More than anything else, it made him want to dance.

Without waking his wife, he crawled from the bed, removed his pajamas, and stepped outside naked, save for a pair of red socks his wife had given him for Christmas the previous year.

Out in the brisk predawn air, he joined his new elf friends in a magical dance up and down the street. And he did his part to make the event a complete success by dancing up to each door on the block and, holding one nostril shut with an index finger, blowing a thick line of snot onto the doorknob. He was having a most delightful time until one of his neighbors, suffering from a bout of insomnia, peeked out the window to see where that strange sound was coming from.

Twenty minutes later, Milton was informed by two uniformed police officers that, unlike his little elf friends, he wasn't invisible.

Rancid, the Devil Horse

*Y*ears ago, in a tri-state area far, far away, there lived a horse named Rancid who worked the traveling pony ride circuit.

Now, at first, "Rancid" might seem a pretty inappropriate name for a pony ride horsey. You'd more likely expect something along the lines of "Checkers" or maybe "Daisy." Something nice for the kids. Swear to God, though, "Rancid" was his given name. Let me explain. See, Bob Mayhem was a horse breeder whose job it was to create world-class racehorses.

Bob, I'm afraid, wasn't that bright, at least when it came to genetics. When he put two of his favorites out in the field together, he was sure the resulting foal would outshine Secretariat.

Problem was, see, neither Ran Outa Gas nor El Cid had ever won a race. Not a one. Never even placed. But Bob, like I said, was a little shaky science-wise, and he figured that since neither one of those horses had ever won a race, their offspring would be unbeatable. (It's not clear what brought him to this conclusion but something did.)

These Children Who Come at You with Knives

When El Cid gave birth that spring Bob, like most horse breeders, chose a name that would reflect the lineage. By combining "Ran Outa Gas" with "El Cid," what else could he come up with? So the young horse was christened Rancid.

It was clear early on that Rancid wasn't cut out to be a racehorse. He had neither the speed, nor the stamina, nor the temperament for the sport of kings. When you get right down to it, Rancid just didn't seem to give a good goddamn about running fast.

Bob, furious that the colt didn't bear out his cockamamie theory, sold Rancid to a two-bit "entertainment promoter," thus banishing him to a life of giving ten minute rides to six-year-olds.

One day in some small town or another, Rancid (and four other young, world-weary horses) trudged round and round a small dirt track bearing a screaming pygmy astride his aching spine.

It wasn't long before young Rancid came to hate people. Every last one of them, from the skeevy, neglectful drug addict who operated the pony ride concession, to the insipid, indulgent parents with their goddamned Instamatics, to those pint-sized cretins who were always yanking his tail, pulling on his ears, kicking at his ribs with their sharp little heels, or leaving lollipops and gum in his mane.

Realizing that his tail was fine for brushing away flies, but of no use whatsoever when it came to keeping away snot-nosed kids, he came up with a better idea.

It was after he threw his third toddler in as many days that Rancid was finally retired. Yet though he was now free of the children, his hatred for people in general persisted and grew. He bit everyone who came near him—even those who were just trying to brush him or feed him carrots and sugar cubes.

"Why don't they ever bring whiskey or chaw?" he fumed. "Do I *look* like I want a carrot? Did I ever *ask* for a carrot? Stupid dickwhacks."

Finally, late one evening, having had enough of being cooped up in the filthy stable with a bunch of broken-spirited horses— he was not only angry but *bored* and angry—Rancid reached over the gate, picked the lock, and slowly galloped away into the night.

That was the thing about Rancid. He might've been a lousy racehorse and even worse when it came to giving pony rides, but he had plenty of other skills. Had Bob Mayhem realized this, he might've thought twice before selling him off for a measly seventy-five bucks.

Rancid, see, was not only ornery, he was smart too. He was remarkably dexterous with his hooves, he understood human language, and best of all he knew what people feared. He made that Mr. Ed look like a big retard, and Francis the Talking Mule look like . . . well, an even *bigger* retard, I guess.

First thing he needed, he knew, was a gun. So Rancid trotted into the nearest town, found the local gun shop, and kicked in the plate-glass window with his hind legs. He grabbed all the guns he could carry and vanished long before the local cops could respond to the alarm.

Three days later, an unusually tall man with a mustache, sunglasses, and a broad-brimmed hat walked into the Chatta- hoochee National Bank, right there on the corner of Third and

Main. At first he seemed like any other customer (if a bit taller), but as he approached the teller's window he pulled a gun.

"Gimme all the cash," the robber demanded, "and no one will get hurt." (It was later reported that the man had a heavy British accent.) The teller, having no interest in getting hurt, quickly complied, handing over a bag full of wrapped bills.

But unlike most bank robbers, who simply grab the cash and flee, the tall man with the mustache grabbed the bag of cash and shot the teller anyway. Then he shot three customers. Only then did he leave the bank, and none too quick either.

Two days after that incident, there was another bank robbery in a town twenty miles away that seemed to follow the same pattern—except this time after being handed the cash, the robber shot the teller, some customers, and the bank manager too.

Difference was, this time the robber wasn't described as a tall man with a mustache and a British accent but rather a chubby Chinaman with a long braid.

Local police were still investigating that second robbery when there was yet a third, over in Potter's Bluff. Five people were left dead by a thief who witnesses insist was a "middle-aged eastern European woman wearing a housedress and a scarf around her head."

Law enforcement officials were stymied. Was it some kind of mass hysteria? A fashionable new trend? Or was it instead a sinister invasion plot? Why else would all these foreigners suddenly be robbing small-town banks and shooting innocent, hardworking Americans if they weren't planning on taking over the country?

It was a little far-fetched maybe, but that last theory was the one most people seemed eager to accept.

It was only after the FBI was called in to help with the investigation that someone noticed something. In each case, all the witnesses insisted that the robber had a tail. Not just a tail but small, pointy ears too. Even the tall British man and the eastern European woman, both of whom were wearing head coverings of some kind, had apparently cut holes to allow the ears to poke out the top.

The case became more baffling by the minute, at least until a still closer examination of the footprints the robber had left while fleeing through the flower garden in front of the Potter's Bluff bank revealed that they weren't footprints at all, but hoofprints.

"Gentlemen," the FBI's field manager for the tri-state area told his agents during their morning briefing the following day, "what we are clearly dealing with here is a horse." He paused for dramatic effect as surveillance camera footage of the first robbery flashed on the screen behind him. "But not just *any* horse. Gentlemen, the horse we're looking for is also a master of disguise. Now look here."

He used a pointer to tap at the image on the screen. "Don't let the mustache fool you. See these pointy ears poking up through the hat? And this mane back here? And if you look carefully . . . I know the picture's a little blurry but look at his knees. Do those look like an Englishman's knees to you?"

An immediate search was undertaken of all the stables in the area. All the circuses, pony rides, carnivals, rodeos, and farms as well. Each of the owners was questioned in depth, and all the horses were counted.

Meanwhile, banks within a fifty-mile radius were robbed by (in order) an Arab, a Mexican, an Irishman, a Swede, and an Eskimo.

It took only a matter of days before the FBI's crack team of investigators came to focus on Rancid, who was referred to publicly only as "a horse of interest."

That was good enough for the nation's tabloids, where he was quickly dubbed "Rancid, the Devil Horse."

"He's like that El Kabong," one slack-jawed twenty-three-year-old was quoted as saying, "but really, y'know, evil."

Soon, people throughout the region began looking at any and every horse they saw with newly born suspicions, and foreigners quickly learned that they'd do best for themselves by avoiding banks.

A massive nationwide manhunt (well, horsehunt) ensued. Rancid's picture was flashed on the news, together with security camera shots from several of the most recent robberies.

Then one day, a nosy do-gooder named Petey was taking his lunch break at a bar in downtown Crumbstock. As he worked on his second beer, Petey took notice of the Canadian sitting a few stools down from him. At least he'd *said* he was Canadian.

More specifically, he'd told the bartender, "Yeah, I'm from Winnipeg, but I like Crumbstock better. Nice people, clean air, plenty of hideouts, convenient, ill-protected banks. All in all, it seems like a good place to raise a family."

This would've normally gone in one ear and out the other, if Petey hadn't at the same time noticed that the Canadian's long tail was hanging over the back of the bar stool.

Thinking twice about trying to grab him or alerting the police right then and there (this was a horse who was packing, after all), Mr. Do-Gooder waited until the "Canadian" downed his fourth whiskey and, a bit unsteadily, prepared to leave. When he did, Petey—who before this never would have been considered a conscientious citizen—followed him from a safe distance.

The Canadian with the tail wandered over to the waterfront area. The entire neighborhood had been abandoned for years, for everyone in town considered it far too dangerous. The timbers of the docks were rotting, the buildings had been condemned, and no one seemed interested in revitalizing it in any way.

Then, as the would-be snitch watched from behind an empty boat shed, the "Canadian" let himself into a dilapidated shack just south of the docks.

Petey had read dozens of newspaper accounts concerning unfortunately hirsute foreigners who had been arrested and soundly beaten by police officers before it was determined that they were not, in fact, evil bank-robbing horses in disguise. Yet for some reason it never occurred to him that he might be mistaken in this case. The moment the door to the shack closed, he whipped out his cell phone, called 911, and whispered to the operator that he'd found Rancid, the Devil Horse's hideout.

Within ten minutes, the place was surrounded by police officers in full riot gear, FBI and ATF agents, a SWAT team, and members of the local militia.

The standoff went on for three hours, with any attempt at negotiations met with several bursts of automatic weapons fire from inside the shack.

Seconds after police were finally able to fire three teargas canisters through the broken front window, the front door flew open and out stumbled what appeared to be a Greek Orthodox priest. Man of the cloth or not, it didn't matter. Half a dozen law enforcement agents—then a few more—pounced on him in a flash. They threw him to the ground and held him there as a few officers snuck in surreptitious kicks to the ribs.

At the same time, several more officers in gas masks stormed into the shack. And, sure enough, inside they found stacks of cash, discarded money bags from banks throughout the area, and a toolbox containing an elaborate and well-stocked disguise kit.

After weeks of searching they knew they'd at last nabbed their horse.

When FBI agents ripped away the tall hat and the fake beard, however, they stopped. One even gasped.

"It's not him," an agent muttered.

Oh, they had their bank-robbing horse all right—they just didn't have the horse they were looking for. They didn't have Rancid. The telltale white spot on the nose gave it away.

Indeed, it wasn't Rancid at all. It was his showboating, drama queen of a younger brother, El Ran Hubbard.

Rancid, see, wasn't in the least interested in robbing banks. What use did he have for money anyway? No, instead, while El Ran Hubbard was playing dress-up, Rancid had become a vicious serial killer, stalking, murdering, and dumping the bodies of dozens of hookers along a thirty-mile stretch of Interstate 219.

He lived happily ever after.

Six-Leggity Beasties

O nce upon a time there was a chubby, slovenly young lad who lived in a very nice three-bedroom apartment with his well-to-do parents.

Billy Crumpley (believe it or not, that was his name: Crumpley) was fourteen years old and, no two ways about it, fat as a pig. He wasn't just "hefty." He wasn't "chunky." He wasn't "big-boned." He was just plain fat. Fatty-fat-fat, even. And he was fat because all he did when he wasn't in school was play video games and eat junk food, usually at the same time. He was none too neat about it either. Wherever he went he left a trail of snack wrappers and crumbs.

His parents, who were of the indulgent variety, said nothing about any of this, fearing they might be stifling the boy in some way, preventing him from reaching his full potential. They went to great lengths to provide him with whatever his little clogged heart might desire.

As a result, Billy had also become a nasty little bugger. He was mean to classmates and teachers and strangers in wheelchairs. He butted in lines, stepped on feet, and shrieked loudly whenever he didn't get what he wanted when he wanted it.

He was a decidedly unpleasant creature. The sad thing about it, though, was he had no idea. That's just the way he'd become, because no one had ever told him any different. His parents didn't say anything, and strangers didn't dare for fear of being sued.

Well, one evening at dinner, Billy's parents informed him that they were taking a little vacation to the Dominican Republic. The catch was that only they were going—Billy was staying home.

"Do you think you can take care of yourself for two weeks?" Billy's father asked. "It's a big responsibility."

"Oh, what do *you* think, stupid? I'm not a baby," Billy told him.

"Just three things we ask of you," his mother said.

"What?" Billy sneered at her, folding his chubby arms.

"You have to go to school as always," she said. "You have to keep the apartment clean. And we'd like you to eat regular meals."

"Right," Billy said, rolling his eyes.

"All we ask is that you *try*," she said. "Your father and I will leave you plenty of money. You could order out from any of the nice places around here."

"Fine," Billy said, wishing they'd just leave already.

"And if there's any trouble," his father added, "be sure and ask one of the neighbors for help."

The thing was, as a result of Billy's appalling behavior,

most of his neighbors wanted nothing to do with him. The only neighbor who didn't completely shun Billy was Bubbles LaVoom, the witch who lived in the apartment next door. She was rumored to be well into her eighties but didn't look a day over thirty-two. Some said this was the result of cosmetic surgery, while others had ideas of their own. Although she was a witch who long ago had mastered the black arts, she was nice to everybody and always tried to help out however she could. She was even nice to Billy, though her efforts rarely achieved the desired effect.

One morning as Billy was locking his door behind him on the way to school, Bubbles LaVoom stepped off the elevator with a bag of groceries.

"Good morning, young Mr. Crumpley," she said brightly as she reached for her own keys. "It certainly is a lovely day outside."

"Yeah, you just do that then," he snarled as he stomped past her. He hated going to school. He hated going outside. Let's face it, Billy hated moving. It made him breathe hard.

The day after his parents had left for the Dominican Republic, Billy came home from school (yes, he actually went) and opened the refrigerator to get a soda. That's when he noticed a cockroach on the floor. After crushing it under his shoe, he thought it was strange to see a roach.

Although he left crumbs and spills and smears of jelly or chocolate on whatever he touched, Billy had never before encountered a roach in the apartment. It wasn't important, and he forgot about it as soon as he was in front of his game again.

As for the three simple things his parents asked him to do while they were away, let's just say they didn't last very long. Oh, he went to school once in a while, so long as he felt like it and as long as he wasn't on a roll with one of his games.

After they left, he took the money they'd given him and loaded up on cases of soda, boxes of cookies, corn chips, cheese curlies, fried pork rinds, candy bars, and donuts.

The "keeping the place clean" rule, well, you can imagine.

As the days progressed, Billy Crumpley began to notice more roaches. He saw them on the floor near his unmade bed, in the bathroom, on the kitchen counter, and crawling around on some of the abandoned snack wrappers that were piling up around the couch. Even these he dismissed as simply a necessary evil, part of living in a big city. Everybody has them. His parents would deal with them when they got back.

Soon, as the cockroaches began appearing in his open bottles of soda and in his boxes of cookies, Billy began to notice something else. A sharp, unpleasant odor had arisen in the apartment. It wasn't garbage or rotting food—he was well familiar with what those smelled like and, besides, his parents had taken the trash out just before they left.

No, this smelled more like piss. But that didn't make any sense—there were no pets around who might have been responsible, and he certainly hadn't had any accidents of his own. Nothing major, anyway.

One of the strangest things about the odor was that it seemed to be localized. It may have spread throughout the entire apartment, but it was most definitely coming from one corner of the kitchen. Yet there was nothing in the corner that should smell like that. Just a small milk crate filled with plastic bags. His parents kept saying they were going to recycle them or something, but they'd been there for years.

The smell started getting so bad that Billy could barely concentrate on the third level of Baby Impaler IV. It got so bad, in fact, that he did something he had never, ever done before. On Saturday morning, he filled a bucket with warm water, soap, and bleach. Then he got a brush his mom kept under the sink and scrubbed the floor in that smelly corner. That was all—just the small corner. It was as far as he could go. He was breathing too hard and sweating too much, and he certainly didn't have the energy to go any further. He wanted only to get rid of the terrible smell, which had been growing worse by the day.

Within an hour the smell was back.

He sprayed some of his mom's aerosol air fresheners everywhere, but that only made his head hurt worse. He opened all the windows but that didn't help either. He became so consumed with the stench of piss that he even forgot about the roaches, who could now be found on the walls, in his shoes, in the sink, and perched on his toothbrush. A few scampered across the television screen while he was playing his game, and he tried to zap them, thinking they were part of the next level. There were dozens, perhaps hundreds of them in the kitchen cabinets, on the plates and the glasses and the five-year-old bag of flour his mom had opened once but never used.

These Children Who Come at You with Knives

As he reached to shove a cookie box into an overfull garbage bag one day, half a dozen brown bugs, each easily two inches long, swarmed out of the trash and over his hands and arms before dropping to the floor and scurrying away. What had been merely a mild annoyance at first was fast becoming an invasion force. They were everywhere he looked and on everything he touched. They didn't even run from the light anymore, boldly and openly going about their business at all hours of the day and night.

Next time he went to the store for some frozen pizzas, he actually bought some roach traps and placed them around the apartment, but they had no discernible effect on the growing infestation.

That wasn't his immediate concern, though. He needed to find the source of the terrible reek and get rid of it. His head hurt and he was feeling sick all the time. Even when he left the apartment and went outside it was all he could taste. For the first time in his life, Billy began feeling a strange new emotion. It was like fear, but not exactly. What it boiled down to was this: he knew he had to get rid of the smell and the bugs before his parents got home or he could be in trouble.

Finally, one evening, something occurred to him. Something that, much to his surprise, had never occurred to him before.

He walked into the kitchen, crushing several unlucky vermin underfoot, and peered into the smelly corner again.

For all the scrubbing and bleaching he'd done in that corner, he had never once touched the crate full of plastic bags. "This can't be it," he thought. "They're plastic."

Now, for the first time in the thirteen years since he and his parents had moved into the apartment, he picked up the crate and looked beneath it.

What should've been a clean patch of white tile floor looked more like one of Braque's early cubist paintings (though of course Billy had heard of neither Braque nor cubism). It was a carpet of brown and black, with no white tile visible at all. Before he could tell himself that it was merely grime that had collected under the crate over the years, he noticed that the outer edges of the brown and black patch were *moving*. A few of the several thousand cockroaches clustered there skittered for safety under the nearby stove.

"*Gaahhh!*" Billy Crumpley said.

Then the plastic crate he was holding in his hands exploded with thousands more insects, which, disturbed from their daily routine, crawled from between and beneath and within the old bags, fleeing up Billy's arms, some into his shirt, others up his neck and toward his eyes, mouth, and hair, others down into his pants.

"*Gaahhh!*" Billy repeated. But now at last he understood where the fetid odor had come from. Over the years the cock-roaches had set up their own community in the plastic crate. It was dark, it was rarely disturbed, and how many times had Billy thrown old soda bottles, half eaten sandwiches, or other food in there when he didn't feel like walking the three extra steps to the trash can?

Whimpering quietly like a puppy and numb from horror, Billy held the crate at arm's length as he backed toward the apartment door. He felt the soft crunching of a hundred tiny exoskeletons beneath his stocking feet.

He opened the door and tossed the crate into the hallway, then he slammed and locked the door.

Unbeknownst to Billy, even before he disturbed the first nest, the roaches—now approaching three million in number—had ventured away from home, setting up other nests under his sink and bathtub, in the walls and behind the bookcase.

Along with feeling something that was almost like fear, Billy also began experiencing another new emotion, which—though he couldn't put a name to it—was something akin to remorse.

Making things worse, his parents were due back in just a couple of days.

No matter how many times he washed the floor where the crate once rested, and no matter how many roach traps he put out, they were still there in growing numbers. No matter how careful he was, he could no longer enjoy a snack without finding one or often more roaches in his food.

At last he broke down and logged on to the Internet. Billy looked up "exterminators" and called the first one on the list. He had no idea how he'd pay for it but it needed to be done.

The man at AAA Exterminators listened patiently to the whimpering young boy on the other end of the phone, taking notes as the kid laid out his story. When he asked for Billy's name, however, he stopped.

"Crumpley?" he snapped. "Up on North Seventieth Street?"

"Yes, uh-huh," Billy said, relieved that his troubles would soon come to an end, even if it seemed a little odd that the exterminator knew where he lived before Billy had told him. He reached up to scratch his head and found another roach nestled in his hair.

"You're the fat kid, right?"

"Huh?" Billy asked.

"Yeah, you're the fat kid. I can hear it. Well let me tell you something, *tubby,*" the exterminator said. "I know all about you. My mom lives on that block, and you once ran right into her. And not only did you not apologize, you called her a name I will not repeat aloud. So fuck your roaches, and fuck *you,* too, you asshole blubberpot. You're a mean, mean little boy and you're getting what you deserve. And you know what else?"

Billy, quite stunned by this, could only ask, "What?"

"I know every exterminator in town, and I'm going to make sure that *none* of them helps you, no matter how much money your rich mommy and daddy offer!"

"I—" Billy began, but the exterminator had already slammed down his phone. What was going on? Nobody had ever talked to him that way before.

As Billy methodically called every other exterminator in town, they either laughed at him or called him names.

He hung up the phone after the last exterminator had called him a "rotten fat-assed poophead." He didn't know what else he could do. He scratched at his legs and his arms even though, for once, there were no roaches there.

Normally, Billy's first reaction would be to insist that his parents sue each and every one of them as soon as they got home, but that didn't occur to him now.

After a long and sleepless night marked by lots of random scratching, Billy Crumpley got up and prepared for school. For once, he was looking forward to getting out of the apartment.

Much as he loathed the evil critters that had taken over his home, the more he lived among them, the more he began to consider something. (This, too, was quite new for Billy.) For the very first time ever, Billy began trying to look at things from someone else's perspective.

These cockroaches, Billy surmised, had no real conception of him. They didn't know why he hated them, or even that he hated them at all. They were interested in merely finding food, finding water, and making more roaches.

What's more, their entire, vast world—the tile floor, the countertops, the sink—was only a tiny part of Billy's own. The world they knew was all they needed to know, and they probably didn't make very much of it. It was what they had, so that's what they worked with.

They probably didn't even make much of the fact that, whenever Billy showed up on the scene, dozens of them tended to die. They didn't know anything about him or his life. He was simply a force of nature to them, maybe even a god. Not only did they not understand a damn thing about him, they were *incapable*, by the very nature of their construction, of understanding anything about him. They weren't evil—they were simply working on instincts determined by their primitive nervous systems. At least that's what he learned in Mr. Adamson's life science class.

In spite of all that, he still knew he had to get rid of the roaches before his parents got home or he'd be in deep shit.

As he was locking the door behind him the next morning on his way to school, Billy noticed that someone had pushed the crate with the plastic bags to the far end of the hall. Behind him he heard a voice.

"How-do there, young Mr. Crumpley? It's another beautiful day outside, and I certainly hope you're able to make the most of it."

It was Ms. LaVoom the witch. She was smiling at him, and in her hand was a small, clear plastic bag filled with herbs and roots of some kind.

Billy noticed the roach crawling up his shirt, brushed it to the ground, and squashed it. Then he put his head down and headed for the elevator. He didn't know what else to do or say.

On his way to the bus stop, however, he felt bad for being rude. He also began to wonder if his neighbor the witch—the witch who had always been nice to him, no matter how snotty he was—just might be the answer to his problems. She could certainly cast a spell or give him some magic powder or something to get rid of the scourge. That's just the sort of thing witches did.

At school, Billy thought of the best way to go about approaching her. He guessed he would have to apologize first. That'd be another new one for him. Perhaps he would even bring her a present. But what do you bring to a witch? Or even a lady, for that matter? He wondered if maybe she liked pork rinds.

On his way home from school, Billy stopped at the bodega for another economy-sized bag of corn chips. Not exactly knowing what a witch might like, he also picked up a small bunch of posies tied with a rubber band and wrapped in green cellophane. People on the TV were giving ladies flowers all the time.

Billy was nervous and scared but he knew it had to be done.

At home, he made a sandwich and ate it standing up, as had become his habit, in an effort to keep the roaches to a minimum. Then he shook the flowers to make sure they were roach-free, stepped into the hall, and hesitantly knocked on Ms. LaVoom's door.

As he knocked, he realized in a moment of panic that he had never decided on the proper way to approach a witch on matters of business. Quickly he began to rehearse, calling up all the things he'd seen and heard in the games he played and the books his mom had read to him when he was real little.

" 'Oh, most great and powerful witch, thy powers are known far and wide, as well as thy great and kind . . .' No, that wouldn't do. 'Pray tell, oh fair witch, wouldst thou deign to show pity upon this poor mortal . . .' Shit. 'Madam, whose powers are the stuff of legend, I, a young man, do seek your wise counsel and aid in matters most . . .' "

He heard the lock turn, then the door opened. Bubbles LaVoom smiled warmly upon finding her young neighbor standing there.

"Why Billy, such a surprise," she said, sounding quite sincere. "And such a pleasure to see you. Won't you come in?"

Her large black eyes were surrounded by a pale face, which, though youthful, still bore a few wrinkles. She had long black hair streaked with either gray or blond (he couldn't tell), and she wore a long, shapeless black dress that was either fashionably tattered or merely tattered (he couldn't tell that either). Around her neck hung a silver pendant that appeared to be a snake curled around an upside-down cross.

"Well, I . . . I . . . I just . . . ," Billy began. "I just wanted, umm . . ."

"Yes?" she asked, stepping back to allow him to come inside whenever he decided to do so.

Finally, still standing in the hall clutching a bunch of flowers in a sweaty fist, he blurted, "I hear that your witchery's really out of this world, Ms. LaVoom . . . Really."

She said nothing, still holding the door open.

"It's just that . . . ," he said hesitantly, then stopped. In his frustration he thrust the flowers toward her. "Here."

"Oh," she said, still smiling. "How very sweet of you."

"I just wanted to say I'm real sorry," he finally forced out. "You've always been very nice. I'm very sorry if I've been mean. And . . . and I wanted to thank you for being nice."

"Please do come in, Billy," she said, taking the flowers and his hand at the same time and pulling him inside, closing the door behind him. "That's not all you came here for, is it?"

"That's mostly it, yeah," Billy said, blushing, finding himself quite unexpectedly inside the apartment. Apart from a few glowing candles, it was completely dark.

"Don't lie to me, Billy," she said, though there was no sharpness to her voice. "I'm a witch and it won't work. You need Bubbles LaVoom's help, yes?"

"Well . . ."

As his eyes slowly adjusted to the light, he began to look around her apartment. He knew for a fact that her apartment was the same size and had the same floor plan as his own, but even those two given facts seemed hard to believe.

– 147 –

The walls, the ceiling, and the floor had all been painted jet black. Even the windows had been painted over black. He caught the reflection of an enormous silver pentagram painted on one wall, and on the floor beneath it stood a circle of red candles. Within the circle of candles sat what appeared to Billy to be a pig's head.

The other walls were lined with shelves, the shelves themselves loaded with colored jars and bottles. One near the top contained what looked to be the fetus of a creature with a tail and three heads. Another jar was labeled, simply, "Flesh." A human skull sat on an ornate desk, and a small plastic bucket next to the skull held an array of what were clearly thin bones. It was just like something out of one of his games.

"Cool," he thought.

The air was heavy with an odor Billy couldn't begin to identify—part incense and part burned meat. It wasn't altogether unpleasant but would probably get there if he hung around too long.

"I knew she was a real witch," he thought, "but I had no idea she was this *much* of a witch."

"So," his host said, startling him, "how might Bubbles be of service?" Her voice remained quite pleasant.

"Well, Ms. LaVoom," he began. "First, again, please let me apologize for being rude in the past. I don't mean to be—it just comes out."

"That's all right," she assured him. "Living in this city can make people do things they may not do otherwise. Things they don't fully comprehend. It can make them downright subhuman."

"Yeah," he said, not really sure what she was talking about. "Ms. LaVoom, I don't know what else to do. The bugs—roaches— have taken over my parents' apartment, and they're gone—my parents, I mean—but they're coming back day after tomorrow. See? I've tried everything: the traps and exterminators. I found their nest and got rid of it but that didn't help." He tried to hold back the tears welling up in his eyes. "I was hoping that you might have something—a powder or a spell or something—that could help me get rid of them. I have to do something—take care of it—before they get back or they'll be real mad." He felt his throat tighten.

"Ahh!" she exclaimed. "Six-leggity beasties and things that go *skitter skitter skitter* in the night!" She tickled her long finger- nails up his arm as she said this. He snapped his arm away and scratched at it, and she laughed. "Of course I can help you. I am a witch, after all. You should've come to me sooner."

"Oh thank you, *thank* you, Ms. LaVoom!" Billy exclaimed, tempted to fall to his knees and hug her legs. "I'm so grateful." Again, he felt the beginnings of tears. These, however, were tears of relief. And beneath the tears he felt some amazement at the fact that he was actually *talking* this way.

"Let me whip something up. It'll just take a jiffy. You wait right there." With smooth, silent steps she strode to the shelves and began pulling down jars. Although he had never seen her put them anyplace, the flowers were now gone.

"That crate," she asked over her shoulder. "The one in the hallway. That was the nest you mentioned?"

"Y-yes," he said. "It took me forever to find it."

"I smelled it out there," she told him as she carried several jars whose labels he could not read toward the kitchen. "I knew immediately that you were having troubles of some kind or another."

He stood and waited where she told him, looking around at the wax-lit apartment as he listened to the sounds coming from the kitchen. He thought she was singing or chanting to herself, but the words were inaudible. He was afraid to touch anything.

"One thing," he shouted in her direction. "Umm, I don't know that I can . . . umm . . . really *pay* you anything right now." It was something that had only then occurred to him. "But I know that as soon as my parents come back, they'll give you . . . you know, whatever." He was starting to worry. Would she want one of his fingers? Would he be asked to sacrifice a baby? He had no idea.

"Oh," her voice came from the kitchen. "That's very simple. From now on, when you see me in the hallway, smile and say hello. That would be more than enough payment. We are, after all, neighbors, so just act neighborly."

Relief melted through Billy's body. He'd get to keep his fingers and he wouldn't have to kidnap and murder anybody's kid. And his parents won't know a thing. "I think that can be arranged," he said. "Sure thing. Thank you for your kindness, Ms. LaVoom. I really can't thank you enough."

A moment later she returned holding a large pewter goblet. It wasn't smoking, as he expected it to be, but the contents were an unpleasant, brackish green. It smelled like cow dung and spoiled milk, with a hint of peppermint. She handed it to him.

"Drink this," she said, "and I assure you that the bugs will leave you alone. They'll stay as far away from you as they can."

"Drink it?" he asked, confused. "Are you sure? I . . . I thought getting rid of the bugs would involve a spell or something, you know? A powder I'd sprinkle around. Not something I drank myself."

"As you said," she explained with great patience, "you aren't familiar with this sort of thing. Trust me. This will do the trick, and quickly too. Spells can take weeks, even years to work."

He held up the goblet and smelled it again, wrinkling his nose and frowning. "Well, if you say so." His stomach convulsed once, but he brought the potion to his lips and drank. He had no real choice in the matter.

"There you go," she said. "Drink it all."

This he did, fighting back the urge to vomit. Much to his surprise, he got it down and was able to keep it there. When he was finished, he smiled proudly and handed the goblet back to her. "That's it? That's all I have to do?"

"That's it," she said, smiling in return. "In a few moments, your problems with the roaches will be a thing of the past."

Billy shook his head in pleasant disbelief. "I sure don't understand it, but I'll accept it, and thank you again for it. You're the witch here after all, right?" He chuckled weakly.

Then he noticed something shifting in her eyes, and her smile turned wicked. "I am indeed the witch here, and there's no need to thank me," she said. "You deserve it. In fact, we all do."

"Huh?" he asked, as he noticed the first tremors. Something was going wrong. He knew it must be his eyes probably still trying to adjust to the darkness, but Ms. LaVoom suddenly seemed a bit taller than she had been a few minutes earlier.

"That roach nest you threw out into the hallway," she explained, "not only made the entire hallway stink of urine—it still does, if you'd bothered to notice—but it released thousands of roaches, which quickly infested every apartment on this floor. This building has never had a roach problem before."

"But, but how can . . . No, no, that's not true—" He tried to protest, tried to ask her where his roaches had come from if not somewhere in the building, to tell her that it couldn't possibly be his fault. But his brain was too busy trying to comprehend what was happening to him. Not only was Ms. LaVoom growing larger—so was the apartment itself. Her face, too, was changing. Her dark eyes shriveled, leaving empty sockets, and her smile now revealed a mouth full of fangs. What had been the attractive face of a woman in her thirties was now a monster's skull.

His own body was changing as well. Something was very definitely going very wrong. His skin felt almost hard. He could hear soft crackling sounds coming from inside. He looked at his hands in time to see the fingers fuse together. He tried to scream as two other appendages burst from his torso. *What has she done to me?* a terrified Billy wondered. *What did you do to me?*

"You've never been anything but a spoiled little pest and a blight on this building," she said coldly as the black, hollow sockets stared down at him. "You apologized to me only because you *wanted* something. That's the way you work. Scream and pout and shove. But you know what?"

He tried to answer but his mouth had vanished. Two long

tendrils had erupted from above his eyes. He was down on the floor now. His flesh had ossified and his internal skeleton had jellied. Everything around him had become enormous, the black ceiling miles and miles above him. Her voice echoed, filling the world.

"It's bullshit. You could be polite, you could be decent if you wanted to—you just don't bother. Your parents have taught you how to get what you want, even if it means hurting people who didn't deserve it. And you will always be that way. It's too late. You are beyond redemption."

He tried to tell her that she was dead wrong about that, but he couldn't form the words. The transformation was almost complete. Billy, now a mere inch and a half long, was nearly insane with confusion and terror. He didn't know what to do, where to go (though under that desk over there seemed a decent choice), or even how to make six legs work together.

"Now you're down where you belong," said a voice that seemed to penetrate his entire body. "Along with the rest of your kind."

Contrary to the theory he had been toying with over the previous few days, Billy understood with the deepest clarity what that giant shoe was, who it belonged to, and what it was about to do to him.

Maggot in a Red Sombrero

*W*ay up on the thirteenth floor of a low-income housing project in a faraway city, there once lived a kindly but poor old widow named Vaselina Honnegger. Poor as she was, she always found a way to get along rather comfortably. Comfortably for her, at least.

Relying on monthly social security checks and the small savings left behind after her husband of forty-seven years was run over (twice) by a school bus, Vaselina lived frugally, allowed herself no extravagances.

But after many years, a diet of boiled grains and watery broth, despite how regular it kept her, left her feeling unsatisfied. She craved something different, something more. Specifically, she craved meat.

So for the next several months she scrimped and saved, denying herself even more than usual until she had enough to go to the supermarket and buy herself a pound of ground chuck.

She hurried home with her precious cargo and placed it in the refrigerator.

To Vaselina, red meat was far too valuable a commodity to cook and eat all at once. That would be wasteful. She had to make it last.

That night, she scraped off a spoonful of the meat, patted it out flat in her thin and leathery hands, seasoned it with a little salt and pepper, then fried it up. It was the size of a Kennedy half dollar, but she thought it was the most glorious and satisfying meal she'd ever eaten. If she were to continue using only a small amount at a time, she thought, she would be able to stretch out the meat for weeks, perhaps even a month or more.

There was one small thing poor Vaselina hadn't considered, however: it was summertime.

In fact, as it happens, it was one of the hottest summers in recent memory. Not only was her apartment not air-conditioned but, living as she did in a housing project, the electricity was a bit spotty, thanks to all the people—not only in the building but throughout the city—who *did* have air conditioners.

Sure enough, one sultry evening less than a week after she'd bought the meat (she'd used only an ounce or so by this time), everything blinked twice, then went dark. She waited a moment for the lights to blink back on, but they didn't. The power was out and it stayed that way.

Vaselina hobbled around the small apartment, trying to figure out what to do. There wasn't much else in the refrigerator—certainly nothing that would spoil—but the meat. The precious, precious meat! She placed it in the freezer, hoping this at least would keep it cold until the electricity was restored.

The hours wore on. Then the days. She didn't dare open the freezer door, fearing that whatever chill was still trapped in there might escape, praying the meat didn't rot. It had taken her so long to save up for it, and she simply couldn't bear the thought of throwing it away.

Then, on the third day, the lights flickered back on, her small radio crackled back to life, and the tiny clock on her bedstand began counting the slow hours again. Vaselina went into the kitchen where, glory be, the refrigerator was humming once more. With fear and anticipation in her old heart she opened the freezer door just a crack. The air was not still cool, as she'd hoped. It was as warm as the rest of the refrigerator—and it smelled mildly rancid.

With heartbroken tears running down her hollow cheeks, she reached inside, pulled out the plate that held the ground chuck, set it gingerly on the counter, and examined the damage.

It wasn't a complete loss, she didn't think. There were some green, fuzzy patches, and a few that were dry and white, but maybe if she scraped off the surface she just might be able to save most of what was left underneath.

She opened a drawer, pulled out a dull butter knife, and began cutting the bad parts away.

When she was finished and all the bad patches had been removed, only a small ball of red, untainted ground beef remained. Two or three ounces at most. It was enough to last her at least a few more days.

Vaselina was staring down at what was left of the meat, thinking she should get it back in the refrigerator before that went bad, too, when she noticed something. A small movement.

She thought it was just her eyes playing tricks at first, still blurred as they were from her tears. But after she shook her head and wiped her eyes she saw the movement again, just under the surface of the beef. Something seemed to be burrowing through it.

Suddenly, a small white worm popped straight out the top. A worm, she couldn't help but notice, wearing a tiny red sombrero.

"Hello!" the worm said.

"*Agk!*" Vaselina replied, recoiling in terror.

"Oh, heavens," the worm said, as he tilted back to peer at her from beneath the wide brim of his red sombrero. "Didn't mean to startle you."

Vaselina by this time had backed up against the refrigerator and was feeling around for anything she might use as a weapon to crush the filthy thing. She'd already put the butter knife in the sink, which was too far away.

Her fumbling old fingers didn't go unnoticed by the intruder. "Please don't do that," he said. "I really don't mean you any harm. I'm new here, see, and was just trying to make your acquaintance."

Strange as it all was, Vaselina couldn't help but notice how very polite the repulsive, wriggling vermin seemed.

"Who-who are you?" she asked, trying to keep the tremble out of her voice. "And, if I may, *what* are you?"

"Well," the slimy white creature said, "I guess I'm a common, ordinary maggot. And I'm very pleased to meet you." Then he squeaked a laugh. "Get it? *Meat?*"

Now, as we all know—and Vaselina knew as well—there's

nothing common or ordinary about a talking maggot wearing a sombrero. Especially when it's in your kitchen. She'd never heard of such a thing in all her life, and told him as much.

"Then I guess that makes us even," the maggot replied, "since I've never heard of a creature like you before either, let alone one in a faded pink bathrobe."

Vaselina looked down at herself, then back at the maggot. Despite the fact that he was sticking out of what little was left of her beloved ground chuck, she felt her initial horror melting away.

"My name's Vaselina," she said hesitantly. "Vaselina Honnegger . . . and you're in my beef."

The maggot looked around himself. "And so I am," he said. "Let me take care of that first off."

With a wriggle this way and a wriggle that way, his long, slick body slithered and slurped out of the raw meat, then slid down to the plate. "There," he said. "So sorry for any inconvenience."

The strangest thing of all about this was that Vaselina, within two minutes of having met a talking maggot wearing a hat—and one who spelled the end of the meat she so cherished—began feeling a softness in her heart for him. How could she hate and fear a creature, even one as disgusting as this, who was behaving so sociably?

It may have been because she was so desperately lonely. She had no family, and all of her friends had long since passed away. She had no one left to talk to, except for occasional telemarketers who, a few short minutes after getting her on the phone, usually made some excuse or another and hung up. (It's also entirely possible that the softness in her heart for the maggot might have had something to do with the onset of dementia, but that's not for us to say.)

Vaselina had never had a pet of any kind before, not even as a young girl, and this maggot seemed so polite and good-natured. Perhaps he could stay with her and keep her company. She didn't know of anything in the lease that said you couldn't keep a talking maggot. And even if there was, nobody paid much attention to anything in those leases anyway.

Vaselina excused herself, got a small chair from the other room, set it down by the counter, and began chatting with the maggot.

"So," he asked after a bit, "you're not going to squash me?"

"Oh my, no!" she told him. "How could I squash such a smart and polite creature as yourself?"

"I'm much obliged," the maggot said. "And if I had arms and hands like you, I'd tip my hat to your generosity and inner beauty." Vaselina felt a blush creep across her face for the first time in thirty years.

On and on they talked, well into the night. Occasionally, the maggot would stretch over and take a small bite of the meat, but Vaselina no longer cared about that. Having someone to talk to was much more important than preserving such an extravagance. Her craving had been fulfilled anyway, and she could go back to boiled grains and broth.

At one point she asked him, "Are you a magic maggot?" It was something she had been curious about as soon as he appeared. After all, a talking maggot wearing a sombrero had to have something else going on.

"Hmmm," he said. "Not that I'm aware of, I'm afraid. But like I said, I'm new here. Who knows what I might be able to do?"

The two agreed quite happily that, magic or not, the maggot would live with Vaselina from that moment onward. She picked him up in her cupped hands and gave him a tour of the apartment.

"My goodness!" he said with delight. "This place is enormous! You must be a very lucky and wealthy woman."

"Oh, Mr. Maggot," Vaselina confessed sadly, "I'm afraid I'm neither. Compared with the way most people live, this is a tiny dump, and I'm very, very poor."

"Well," the maggot said, "it certainly seems like a grand palace to me, and I'm more than honored that you'll allow me to live here with you."

The two of them spent their days talking and listening to the radio. The maggot was curious about everything, from appliances and plumbing to the world outside the dirty windows, and Vaselina answered his questions as best she could. She also made a point of bringing him along with her whenever she ran her errands. He accompanied her as she went to the grocery store or down to the corner mailbox. On nice days, they sometimes even took strolls in a nearby park. The maggot, always in his red sombrero, rode on her shoulder and was terribly excited about each new thing he saw.

Checkout clerks at the grocery store and passersby on the street couldn't help but stare at the maggot, usually with faces riddled with shock and horror and disgust. But nobody said anything to Vaselina directly and nobody offered to brush the maggot away, assuming her to be an insane, filthy homeless woman who'd infect them with some noxious disease if they got too close.

Vaselina saw their faces and paid them no mind. They would never understand how very happy she was with her maggot, and how happy he was with her.

There was one small thing she hadn't considered, which, after a time, began to make itself apparent.

Never having had anything akin to a pet in her life (apart from her husband), she forgot all about feeding him.

Oh, in the first days she tried, laying out a small bowl of gruel next to her own and setting the maggot down in front of it, but he showed no interest. After a third day of trying, she decided it would be best to stop wasting perfectly good gruel that way. She knew very little about maggots and so came to the conclusion that maybe they didn't eat after they'd reached a certain stage.

But the maggot was getting mighty hungry. He didn't want to be rude about it given how kind Vaselina had been to him, so phrasing it as carefully as possible one day he said, "You know, I'm getting a mite peckish here. You don't suppose I'd be able to get a little bite to eat, do you?"

"Why certainly you can, Mr. Maggot," she told him, and she carried him into the kitchen. She set him on the countertop, opened the refrigerator door, and removed the pan of watery chicken broth she'd made three nights earlier.

"I'm—I'm sorry," the maggot interrupted. "I'm afraid I can't eat that."

"It's no good?" she asked, bending her nose to the pan and sniffing. "Does it smell bad?"

"No—no, that's not it. It's just that, see, I'm a *maggot*. And as a maggot, I prefer a diet consisting mainly of rotting meat. Decayed flesh of some sort. Do you happen to have any around?"

Vaselina stopped and stared at him for a long time.

"Rotting meat?" she asked.

"Yeah, pretty much. If you don't have any on hand, maybe we could go down to the store and pick up a little something? Then leave it out for a bit?"

"Oh, but Mr. Maggot, meat is so terribly expensive. I just don't have the money to buy any right now."

The maggot's face fell. "But . . . where did you get that meat that was here when I first showed up? You must be able to afford it sometimes."

"I'm sorry, Mr. Maggot," she said. "In order to afford that meat, I had to scrimp and save for a very long time." Then she added sadly, "And it went bad before I could eat very much of it."

"Oh, buck up there, Vaselina," the maggot said with a smile. "Don't be a gloomy gus. You got me out of the deal, didn't you?"

She offered him a tiny smile in return. "Yes, that I did."

"Great. So start saving your money again. I'm famished."

And so she did. After paying her rent and all her monthly bills, Vaselina would set aside a few pennies in a special meat fund.

Every day, the maggot would ask her how much she had saved, and how much longer it would be before she'd be able to buy him some meat.

"A little while yet," she'd explain. "It's very expensive."

As the days and weeks wore on, though, the maggot became more demanding, and Vaselina grew tired of him asking the same damn questions every day when the answers never changed. Soon all they talked about was the ETA of the maggot's meat. Vaselina grew more weary, and the maggot grew hungrier and nastier. He sometimes called her ugly names and accused her of not really wanting to feed him, of wanting to let him starve to death.

"That's not true!" she tried to counter, but he was hearing none of it. She begged him to at least try some of the broth or the gruel in the meantime, just until she had enough saved up, but he refused, sometimes even spitting in the bowls she placed in front of him.

"*I need meat!*" he'd shout in his squeaky maggoty voice. "You hear me? *Putrid, rotting meat!*"

It all became too much for poor Vaselina. She was trying so very hard but it just wasn't good enough. Having someone to talk to was nice, but she'd gotten along before without. Arguing and accusing each other regarding the meat issue all the time was much worse, she felt, than being lonely again.

Quietly at night, as she lay in her bed, her brain began thinking things she'd never thought before—or even thought herself capable of thinking.

How long did maggots live? She didn't know. What if they lived for years or decades or even longer? The thought was too horrible. She had to get rid of this wretched, demanding maggot one way or another. And soon.

You'd think it would be easy, right? Sombrero or not, he was only a maggot. Just pick him up, pinch the guts out of him, wash your hands, and there you go. Maggot problem resolved.

But it wasn't that simple, for you see he was a clever maggot. What's more, unbeknownst to either of them, he did have a hint of magic about him.

One afternoon when she'd taken all she was willing to take and finally reached out a hand to swat him, the maggot vanished a moment before her hand slapped down on the table where he'd been sitting.

Somewhere along the line—perhaps it was nothing but instinctive—he'd learned that if he blinked his eyes and nodded his head a certain way he could disappear, then reappear instantaneously somewhere else. It only worked within a ten-foot radius measured from his starting point, but when you're a maggot that's all you need.

After her hand smacked the table, Vaselina was sure she'd squashed him. Her relief was short-lived, however, as the unmistakable voice behind her sneered, "What in the fuck do you think you're doing?"

She turned and saw the maggot, fresh as a daisy, over near the lamp. She clumsily lunged toward him again, and again he seemed to evaporate in the millisecond before her hand struck him. Instead, she sent the lamp crashing to the floor.

She heard laughter behind her. A bitter, taunting laugh. She turned and saw him on the threadbare couch and lunged again.

On and on it went for most of the afternoon.

"Give it up, lady. Can't you see it's pointless?" he snarled after the first hour. "You should be using all that energy to go buy me some goddamn *meat*."

"I can't *afford* it!" she cried with frustration, but he wouldn't listen.

As evening began to fall outside the apartment windows, both combatants found themselves on the couch, too exhausted to go on like that (magic or not, teleporting was a tiring business, especially on an empty stomach). After some ten minutes of silence, they looked at each other and began to chuckle at their foolishness.

"Look at us," the maggot said. "This is no way for friends to act."

"No," Vaselina said between wheezes, "it certainly is not."

That night they went to sleep and slept well, having put all of their differences behind them.

The calm lasted through the night until seven thirty the following morning, when the maggot started in with her again.

"Even some cheap breakfast links or something, Christ," he muttered as she sipped her weak morning tea. "Look at you. So satisfied. So well fed."

"Why must you constantly torment me like this?" she asked. "Why don't you listen to what I have to say? I'm saving, and as soon as I have enough I'll buy you meat. You have no idea how hard it is!"

She began sobbing, but the maggot just sighed. "All I'm saying, Vaselina, is that this amounts to animal cruelty, your starving me this way."

She looked at him aghast. "Animal cruelty? But you're a *maggot*. You're only barely an animal at all! No one would ever convict me."

"Have you forgotten that I'm a *talking* maggot? I get up there on the stand and tell the jury what's been going on, and you're looking at hard time, believe you me."

She knew he probably had her there.

Then she had an idea. For as long as the torment had been going on, she couldn't believe she'd never thought of it before.

"You're magic," she said. "So why don't you just, you know, blink your way into a butcher shop? You could have all the meat you want, forever and ever. And I could stop fretting about it all the time."

The maggot considered this. The meat wouldn't be rotten (at least if it was a halfway decent butcher shop), but it would be something.

"It's not a bad idea," he said, "as much as it's a difficult one. See, this trick of mine, it's imprecise. I don't know where the hell I'm gonna end up. And as you've seen yourself, I can't go that far at any one time. Just a few feet. I might not ever find my way to a butcher shop."

She sighed in disappointment. Then her eyes brightened again. "I know. I could *take* you to a butcher shop and drop you off inside. How's that?"

"Then leave and be done with me, right? That's your plan?"

"No—"

"Oh, yes it is. I know you. That's exactly what you were thinking. You'd bring me inside, and the moment I got myself burrowed headfirst into a big hunk of rump roast you'd be out the door."

"I swear, I—" Vaselina protested, even though that was pretty much exactly what she was thinking.

The maggot shook his head. "Just cut it. Thing is, I am awful hungry. It might be worth a try, no matter what. But if you abandon me there, believe me, one way or another I'll track you down and make your life a living hell, got it? It might take a while, but you'd regret it in the end, that's for sure."

"Completely understood," Vaselina agreed with a smile. "I'll stay in the shop while you eat, then we'll both come back here and things will be just as good as they used to be."

"Deal," the maggot said, nodding his sombrero vigorously.

Vaselina was so thrilled she could hardly believe it. She would actually be rid of the awful monster once and for all. She felt a rush of bright energy flowing through her veins like she hadn't felt since she was a girl. She hurriedly changed her clothes and began putting on her shoes.

Twenty minutes later the bells above the front door of Crampello's butcher shop tinkled and in walked Vaselina, the maggot safely hidden in her pocket.

She took a look around the small shop. There were only two other customers, and they were keeping the man behind the counter quite busy. It was perfect.

"Here we go," she whispered. She pretended to be browsing in front of the meat case, making sure to keep her back to the other customers. She drew the maggot out of her pocket and let him consider the offerings.

"Man, just *look* at it all," he whispered. Then, after spotting a display of freshly cut sirloins, he was ready. "Okay, here I go." He blinked his eyes, nodded his head, and vanished.

A moment later, instead of appearing behind the glass on top of several mouthwatering steaks, she saw him wriggling on the floor in front of the case.

Vaselina stooped and picked him up before anyone noticed.

"What happened?" she whispered.

"Glass," the maggot hissed, wriggling in pain and still shaking his bruised head. "I guess I can't go through solids. I need a clear and direct line."

Vaselina looked around, still trying to be casual. "So what do we do?"

"Everything's back there?" he asked, nodding at the long display counter.

"Yes, it is."

The maggot thought about it briefly, then said, "Only one thing we can do. You've got to get me back behind the case."

"But . . . I can't do that. He'll see me."

The maggot swallowed an angry bark. *"Listen,"* he told her. "It'll only take a second. Get me back there, I'll blink, and then you come back here, okay? If he says anything, just play stupid. I'll be set by then."

Even though she thought it was a bad and dangerous idea, Vaselina began to sidle down toward the opening at the other end of the counter.

She looked at the butcher. He was a huge bald man wearing a blood-spattered apron. There was no way she could do this.

Then one of the customers asked the butcher for a special cut of veal shank, which meant he had to retreat to the back room for a moment.

Vaselina couldn't believe her good fortune. She breathed a sigh of relief, and as soon as the butcher stepped through the door into the back, she ducked around the counter behind the display case, drew her hand from her pocket again, and the maggot vanished.

"What in the hell d'ya think you're doing?" an enraged voice boomed behind her.

Vaselina turned, eyes wide, to face the blood-smeared butcher, who was now standing in the doorway clutching an unwashed cleaver. "I'm—I'm so sorry," she stammered in a panic as she stood frozen in place. "Y-you were busy, an-and I wanted to see these chops here and—"

One of the customers screamed and pointed.

Everyone looked and saw the maggot perched atop a pile of handmade wieners.

"What in the hell is that!" the butcher bellowed. *"And what's it wearing?"*

"It's a . . . a sombrero," Vaselina offered, trying to be helpful.

The other customers fled the store, and the maggot, fearing for his own safety, reappeared in Vaselina's hand.

"It's yours?" The butcher drew closer. He was still clutching the cleaver. "What in the *fuck* are you trying to do—*ruin* me? Who sent you?"

"No! No! He . . . he just needed to eat. He was—"

"You're fuckin' *crazy*, lady!" He took another step toward her, cleaver raised.

Seconds later they were back on the sidewalk, after being dragged to the front door by the butcher, who informed Vaselina that if she even walked past his shop again she would find herself hanging from a stainless-steel hook in his freezer.

They walked home in silence. The moment the apartment door closed behind them, however, the maggot (who was now more cantankerous than ever) let loose with a torrent of names and accusations.

"It seemed like a good idea," Vaselina offered, her voice weak.

"Good idea, my ass!" the maggot yelled. "And when push came to shove, what did you do? Play it cool? No, first you panicked, then you told him everything. You almost got me *killed*. Thanks a hell of a lot for that one, lady. Some friend you are."

He moved to the other side of the room and continued yelling as Vaselina took off her coat, then sat down to remove her shoes.

"Stupid ass cow!" the maggot shouted.

Vaselina was so very tired after the trip, the stress, the past several days. Worse, she knew the maggot would be yelling like this for the rest of the afternoon. "Why couldn't he just die or something?" she wondered.

As she bent over to remove her left shoe, she felt something. A flutter, then a sharp pain. She put it down to gas at first, but as she tried to stand it became clear that it wasn't gas at all.

Everything that had happened—the exertion, the anxiety, the stress, the unending frustration—came together in a single, terrible instant. Vaselina's weary old heart spasmed twice and seized up. She crumpled to the floor and lay on her side, a bolt of hot pain shearing down her arm and up through her jaw. She wheezed and moaned as her dry fingers clawed feebly at her chest in a futile effort to release the agonizing pressure.

The maggot, who was still yelling at her from across the room, stopped only after she hit the linoleum. He blinked, nodded, and was beside her in an instant.

"Vaselina?" he asked. "C'mon, get up. There's no time for these sorts of shenanigans. We've got work to do . . . C'mon, don't be stupid."

She groaned again, curling her head toward her bent and trembling knees.

"Vaselina?"

Incoherent with the merciless pain ripping through her chest, Vaselina tried to dig her nails into the floor, her eyes shut tight, her legs twitching. Then, not fully aware of what she was doing or why, she snatched up the maggot (who hadn't been paying close attention for once), popped him in her mouth, and swallowed him whole, sombrero and all. It all happened in a matter of seconds.

Then her heart stopped beating forever, her hand flopped to the floor, and her body grew still.

Deep in the humid darkness of her otherwise empty belly, the solid truth of what had just happened slowly began to dawn upon the confused maggot, and, with it, a deep sorrow. He knew where he was, and he knew she was gone. She had been his only friend. Even if she hadn't fed him, she still took (mostly) good care of him and treated him with kindness, while all he could do in response was pester and nag her.

"Oh, what have I done?" he wailed.

Then something occurred to him that at once multiplied his love for her, as well as his anguish. In spite of how poorly he had treated her, Vaselina's final act in this world had been one of overwhelming kindness and generosity—as well as an end to both of their troubles. With a shrug and a quiet prayer of thanks to Vaselina, wherever her spirit might be, the maggot stretched himself out and took a little nibble from the lining of the dead woman's stomach. It was still warm. Then he took a bigger bite. He was delighted to discover that her gastric juices made for an unexpected and quite satisfactory gravy.

I'm happy to report that, from that day on, the little maggot in the red sombrero had more to eat than he'd ever dreamed possible.

Stench, the Crappy Snowman

The first snow of the season fell early on the suburbs that year.

It wasn't a heavy snow, merely a few delicate flakes drifting down from overcast skies. But the flakes fell throughout the night, and by Saturday morning enough of them had gathered to cover the brown, dead blades of grass that, for the previous weeks, had defined the Terwilligers' yard.

There were also enough of them to spark the young enthusiasms of the Terwilliger children, Rosetta and Ronald, who swarmed about their father like two enormous gnats as he attempted without success to enjoy the morning's second cup of coffee.

"Father!" they shrieked in their excitement. "Can we build a snowman?"

Mr. Terwilliger sighed, set his coffee cup down on the kitchen table, and cast a doubtful eye out the window to the backyard.

"I really don't think there's enough snow out there yet," he told them. "If you want to make a really decent snowman, you need lots and lots of snow."

Mr. Terwilliger, who had grown up in northern Minnesota, knew such things. He also knew, much to his great unspoken relief, that it was doubtful they would ever receive enough snow where they were living now to construct a decent snowman.

"Oh, *please?*" Rosetta and Ronald begged, pulling at either sleeve of his bathrobe. "Can we?"

Mr. Terwilliger had known his children long enough to realize that this would continue throughout the morning and well into the afternoon if he didn't relent. He looked out the window again and saw that the snow was still falling, if barely.

"Okay," he finally sighed in defeat, "but it'll have to be a small one. There's just not enough snow out there yet for a big one."

"*No!*" the children protested. "A *big* one! We want a *big* one!"

"All *right*," Mr. Terwilliger told them sharply, while something in his brain told him he was doomed to failure yet again. "We'll make a big one."

"Hooray!" both children exclaimed.

An hour later, overbundled by the neurotic Mrs. Terwilliger in hats and scarves and snowsuits and mittens and extra socks and long underwear and boots, the two Terwilliger children, along with a reluctant Mr. Terwilliger, stepped out the back door and surveyed the prospects.

The sky was gray and sluggish, the air damp and chilly. More than a few blades of dead grass were still poking above the thin layer of snow, and the footprints of several passing dogs revealed the unwelcome layer of wet mud that was already seeping through the meager white blanket.

The Terwilligers lived in a small beige duplex situated at the corner of Fruter and Pratter Streets. Not only were they bound along the front and one side of the house by blacktopped roads, there were sidewalks too. The idea of foot traffic filled Mr. Terwilliger with more dread. He felt exposed. People would see him out there hopelessly attempting to build a snowman out of nothing, like an idiot. People on their way to the drugstore up the street would see him failing again, and they would laugh at him. He just wanted to be done with it as soon as possible.

"We'd better move quickly," he said. "Ronald, you make a snowball and start rolling it around to pick up more snow and make it bigger. Rosetta, you do the same, but not as big. I'll make a smaller one for the head."

The children yipped gleefully and stomped out into the yard, leaving a trail of brown footprints behind them.

An hour later, the three necessary snowballs—large, medium, and small, none of them even vaguely approaching "round"—were complete. This was a good thing, as in the process they'd scraped up all the available snow in the yard. They'd also scraped up a good deal of mud, loose, bristly blades of dead grass, and several other bits of detritus that had been scattered around the lawn.

When the three snowballs were finally, hesitantly, stacked atop one another and stuck together best as could be managed, the finished, lumpy construction stood a full five feet tall. The results were far from the pristine white of the snowmen you see in picture books or on television shows. The Terwilligers' snowman was smeared with black and brown and yellow, with only occasional patches of white showing through. Grass, small chunks of gravel, bits of dead leaves, a few cigarette butts, and one lonely, frozen earthworm were embedded in its snowy flesh.

"Well," Mr. Terwilliger said, relieved more than anything that they were finished and that no one—especially Mrs. Terwilliger—could claim that he hadn't fulfilled his fatherly duties. "He may not be pretty but he's all done, eh, children?"

"But we *aren't* done yet," Rosetta insisted in her sweet four-year-old lisp. "He doesn't have a face. He needs coal eyes and a carrot nose, like in the pictures!"

"And arms!" Ronald added. "And a hat and a scarf like a real snowman!"

Mr. Terwilliger looked down at his two children, the fruit of his loins, both soaked through and covered from head to foot with thick muck and dead grass. He should have known this was coming.

"I see," he said. He knew again that he was beaten. He had to come up with something. But what?

There were no lumps of coal handy (they used gas heat). And a carrot nose would require a trip to the Save-O-Rama, which he was in no mood to undertake. Even tree-branch arms were out of the question, as all the trees in the entire neighborhood were little more than saplings. He looked around in desperation.

"Look," he told them, "everybody makes snowmen with coal and carrots. What say we improvise instead? That would be much more fun."

He was trying, he really was. No one could deny that. But now what? He knew they didn't dare go tromping through the house in the condition they were in, looking for buttons or even that old pair of Groucho glasses he had in his desk drawer. Mrs. Terwilliger would blow a gasket. No, they were stuck out here. They'd have to make do.

"I know!" Rosetta cried, running around toward the front of the house. Ronald and Mr. Terwilliger followed, curious and confused.

Out front, they found Rosetta standing next to the black plastic garbage bag that Mr. Terwilliger had dragged out to the end of the driveway the night before.

"Oh, honey, no," he began weakly. "I really don't think that's such a good idea . . ."

Before any of his words reached her delicate red ears, however, she had thrown off her mittens and set upon the bag, tearing it open with her tiny, sharp fingernails. Soiled napkins and soggy paper towels, coffee grounds, orange rinds, half-eaten TV dinners in folded foil trays, soda bottles, chicken bones, crumpled, sour milk cartons, a broken clock, and wet newspapers spilled out across the driveway. An instant later, both Terwilliger children began pawing through the bounty of potential snowman organs and limbs.

"Oh, children, no—I . . . your mother—" But his protests were in vain. He glanced nervously over his shoulder at the duplex, hoping to God she wasn't watching.

When the children were almost finished, the Terwilliger snowman had arms made from gnawed chicken wings. The left eye was a bent bottle cap, the right the thick green, jagged bottom from the very same bottle that Mr. Terwilliger had smashed against the wall in a fit of pique while watching a football game the previous Sunday. The mouth was a flat, round plumbing seal that had cracked some time ago and finally had been thrown away. More than anything else, the snowman was beginning to resemble a Francis Bacon painting.

All he was missing now was a nose. Mr. Terwilliger knew this full well, but he was hoping beyond hope Rosetta and Ronald hadn't noticed. He was cold and damp and wanted nothing more than to get back inside, clean himself up, and lock himself away in his office alone for the rest of the day.

"Well," he said to his wet, filthy, and now stinky children. "What do you say? Are we finished now?" His voice was noticeably strained.

"Without a nose?" asked a suspicious Rosetta.

"Yeah," Ronald agreed. "How will he smell?"

"How will he . . . ?" Mr. Terwilliger began, then stopped himself and sighed heavily. "Okay, if you two can find him a nose, great. I'll wait here and keep an eye on things."

Having already scavenged what they felt they could from the scattered trash, the children scampered about, scouring the yard and the sidewalk and the curb for anything they might have missed earlier.

Five minutes later Ronald found the perfect nose, given the available choices. He scooped it up in his mittened hand and ran back to the pathetic snowman and their despondent father.

"I've got it!" he announced, holding out the nose.

Mr. Terwilliger, relieved at last to be just about done with the whole miserable ordeal, looked down into the hand of his eight-year-old son, the person who would proudly carry on the family name, and saw a frozen dog turd.

By this point he no longer cared.

"That's a great nose!" he told Ronald.

"Put it in, Father! Put it in and make him complete!"

"Uh . . . tell you what, son," Mr. Terwilliger suggested. "Why don't I give you a boost so *you* can put it in?"

Ignoring the screams from his lower back, that's what he did, wrapping his drippy and filthy son in his arms and hoisting him a foot off the ground. The boy drilled the frozen turd into the middle of the muddy face, where it drooped slightly between the mismatched eyes, pointing downward toward the open and shrieking mouth.

He set the boy down again, surveyed the damage to his spine, then prepared to go inside.

"Wait!" Rosetta cried. "Hat and scarf! Or else he'll get cold!"

"Yes, *fine*," Mr. Terwilliger snapped, snatching the knitted cap from atop Ronald's head and unraveling the sticky, encrusted, once-red scarf from around his neck before slapping them both on the snowman. "*There.*"

Rosetta, recognizing from his voice that it wasn't wise to push her father much further, said meekly, "He needs a name."

Mr. Terwilliger glared at her but said nothing.

After a moment's consideration, Ronald blurted, "He looks like Stan!" He was thinking of their uncle Stan, a man neither child had ever once seen sober or clean. It was a particularly apt name for the new snowman. However, since Ronald had been chewing on the thumb of his mitten when he said this, and because his lips were slightly numbed by the cold, "Stan" came out sounding more like "Stench." Which, as it happens, was also quite appropriate.

"Then Stench it is!" Mr. Terwilliger said, his voice nearly cracking with frustration. As finished with the snowman as he ever intended to be, he quickly herded his children unceremoniously toward the back door before they could think of anything else. Once inside, they would never look at or think of their creation again.

But something happened out in the backyard that dreary gray day. Something none of them had noticed, nor likely would have, even if they'd been paying careful attention.

When the frozen dog turd was drilled into the middle of his face, and the nasty hat and scarf were placed upon his head and around his neck, something magical and mysterious had flickered deep within Stench. It was as if he were slowly awakening from a coma following a horrible automobile accident.

"I'm . . . *alive*?" Stench thought. Then, recognizing that being able to think such a thing meant something, he thought, "Goodness gracious me. I *am* alive!"

That much was true. Stench the snowman was indeed now very much among the living. The joy that accompanied this glorious epiphany was short-lived, however, as he realized almost immediately that he also felt horrible. Something was clearly wrong. He was in terrible, excruciating pain.

Then Stench did what many people in similar situations do: he took inventory.

He began with his legs, only to realize in short order that he had no legs. That was all right—he would make do. He was alive, and that was the important thing. But the more he began to work his way around his body, the more the awful truth began to add up.

The sight in one eye, though distorted, was much better than it was in the other. He noticed an awful smell that seemed inescapable, and his mouth was evidently frozen open in a silent scream. That seemed to make sense. He tried moving his arms, but they were so short and twisted he couldn't even clap his hands.

"My heavens, what is this?" he thought in horror. He tried moving his arms again, but the gnawed chicken wings barely wiggled. "I'm—I'm a Thalidomide baby!"

Stench may not have been a Thalidomide baby in the true medical sense, but he certainly was woefully defective. There was no other way to put it.

An unending wave of violent nausea wracked his innards, his back was killing him, and his head felt like it was full of lava and razor blades. Various independent, savage pains rocketed through his body. And there was that awful, putrid odor that seemed somehow to be trapped within him. If he could have closed his one almost-good eye he would have, just to get some rest. Or better yet, sink into his coma once more and shut out all the agony for a while. But he was awake now, and he knew he would remain that way. He was alive, yes, but being alive like this was a curse, a cruel and vicious joke, a punishment unlike anything any living creature could deserve. Stench wanted to scream, but he was in too much pain even for that.

He stood immobilized and suffering all day and all night in the Terwilligers' backyard, watching the people and the cars and the dogs as they passed by. No one paused to help him. Even if they had, what could they have done?

Initially, he felt loathing for them, all these people he saw. He hated their mobility and their obvious good health. They weren't wracked with agonizing, tortured spasms at every moment, and they weren't trapped. They were *free*. If they wanted to laugh or cry or dance or sleep, they could. Not Stench. He tried to weep once, but it only made things worse.

Then he realized that hating these people for being able to do the things he couldn't was pointless. They were, after all, a different species. They were human and he was a snowman. A miserable, tainted, physically corrupt snowman, perhaps, but still a snowman, who could never be like them.

For a few days he waited, praying he would grow numb to the pain, trying to convince himself that, shrieking torment aside, being a snowman actually made him far superior to these humans somehow. Then he couldn't think of anything to justify such a notion, so he abandoned it.

No, they were just different, was all, and he could not hate them or hold them in contempt because of it.

As he noticed how many of them paused on the sidewalk, or slowed their cars to point and laugh at him, however, he thought that maybe he wouldn't completely give up that "hatred and contempt" idea quite yet. He'd at least keep it handy.

The Terwilliger children never played in the backyard, and no one who walked by ever came close. No one ever waved or smiled at him. Not in a nice way, at least. Not even those few who looked at him with pity in their eyes. No one offered a kind word or a pat on the back. Not even an aspirin. They always kept walking.

Then one day a wandering golden retriever galumphed across the backyard, his tail wagging, barking happily.

"Hello there, boy!" Stench said, as the dog paused and looked up at him with quizzical brown eyes. "You don't think I'm hideous, do you?"

The dog barked again, tail still wagging furiously.

"Good boy!" Stench said. "Why, if I could pet you, I would. These despicable withered arms of mine, see?" He waggled them for effect. "But I sure do like you. You're the first creature, human or otherwise, who's ever been nice to me. I've waited so long for someone to talk to."

The dog barked once more and began sniffing the ground around Stench's wide and misshapen base.

"What'cha doing, huh?" Stench chuckled. "Just getting to know me a little bit? Well you go right ahead. I'm certainly glad to see you too!"

The dog paused, lifted its leg, and pissed on Stench. When it was finished, it bounded away again, back the way it had come.

"Oh," Stench mumbled, as his body shifted slightly to the left, and he slipped once more into deep sorrow.

As the days passed, he often found himself, in the depths of his anguish, praying to the God of the Snowmen to send a blizzard his way. It didn't even have to be a full-fledged blizzard. A simple heavy snow would do. A few inches worth. Anything to give him a fresh, clean coating of white to cover the filth and the crud. Something to make him look pure and nice, something that would hide his afflicted surface. Then, even though he'd undoubtedly still feel miserable and rotten on the inside, he'd at least look unblemished on the outside. That's clearly what mattered to all those people who passed by. They'd stop with their jeers and taunts if only he looked good.

Sadly for Stench, it turned out to be an unseasonably mild winter, and no new snowfalls of any note arrived.

On the days when the sun was out, he'd started to melt a little bit, which only left him looking and feeling worse. It felt like an army of diseased bugs was working its way through his entire system, gnawing and chewing and vomiting as they went. What little white he had shown in the beginning was long gone, as the mud and other vile stains slushed through every flake of him. His head drooped and his body became more grotesque. He even watched in impotent horror one day as the dog turd that was his nose began to thaw and drip.

"Oh, God, no! *Nooooo!*" his mind screamed. "Why do you torture me?" he railed at the God of the Snowmen. "Why do you prolong my anguish this way? What have I done to deserve this?"

The wind howled in response, but there was silence beneath it.

It had been over a month since the day of Stench's accursed birth, and each day it seemed his condition grew more wretched. One of his "arms"—not that it was of any real use to him—had fallen to the ground. His bad eye had done the same. Even his nose, which he had eventually come to accept, if not exactly love, had smeared its way down his face and through his mouth, finally settling into the waiting folds of the filthy scarf beneath his chin.

His nausea and pain had grown to be an agony so intense that it had nearly driven him to the point of complete and utter howling madness.

Late one frigid evening (the cold at least numbed him momentarily), Stench heard a noise coming from behind him.

It was voices. Several of them.

They sounded like teenagers cutting through the backyards. He'd heard people do such things on numerous occasions, but none of them had ever come this close to him before.

The more he listened, the more it became clear. There were three of them, and they were quite drunk.

"Hey," he heard one of them say. "What's that thing?"

For a moment, Stench felt a brief lightness in his spirits. Perhaps they would stop and chat, even offer him some sympathy. Then the teenagers appeared in front of him. There were indeed three of them, and all three were thin and evil-looking, like rats. Narrow faces and tiny eyes. They wore black leather jackets and black stocking caps. With his remaining, distorted eye, Stench saw that one of them was carrying a bottle of wine.

"Why, I do believe this is some sort of snowman. Or *was*, at least."

"You don't say," a second boy said. "Isn't that cute? A *snowman*."

"Pretty crappy snowman, if you ask me," the boy with the wine added. "Look at him. Jesus, he's a mess." Then he began to laugh. "Are you kidding me? Was that his nose?"

All three laughed then, but the middle boy stopped.

"I hate snowmen. They creep me out almost as much as clowns."

"So why don't you do something about it?" the first boy prodded. "It's not like he's going to fight back."

"No, please," Stench thought piteously. "I really don't need this."

"Let's give the little morons who built him something to think about."

The first heavy boot landed in his side.

The boys began whooping, and soon all three were upon Stench. They kicked him and clawed at him with their gloved hands. The one with the bottle even used that to pound repeatedly on poor Stench's skull.

His hat was knocked to the ground, followed by chunks of his head. His mouth was tossed some distance away and his remaining eye was torn out. Now he was completely blind. Pieces of his body were flying every which way as the boys continued to batter at him.

Soon, Stench had collapsed enough that all three boys were on top of him with their boots, stomping him into the earth, breaking the larger pieces into smaller and smaller ones. In a brief, pointless explosion of cheap and drunken cruelty, they reduced the miserable snowman to the diffuse elements that, just a few weeks earlier, had been used to create him.

And that, Stench thought with his final, dim flash of consciousness, was just about the nicest thing anyone had ever done for him.

The Toothpick

In a small and quiet village not far from the sea, there once lived a young fellow by the name of Slim Slinneanach. He wasn't the strongest boy in town, nor the swiftest, nor the cleverest. He wasn't even particularly good looking. But Slim had some big ideas. He knew he was destined for greatness.

He wasn't sure how it would come about or what he'd need to do in order to achieve this, but something told him it was inevitable.

One dreary, overcast summer afternoon during his sixteenth year the idea came to him.

"I need to get out of this podunk town," he thought. "That's the most important thing. Nothing ever happens here."

For the most part this was true. To some outsiders passing through on their way to someplace important, the village might have seemed picturesque and quaint—a fine place to raise a family—but truth be told it was pretty dead. Most of the town's residents worked at the local mill and spent their weekends in their wood-paneled rec rooms, drinking cheap beer and watching sporting events on the television. Those two things—the factory and the sporting events—comprised the two primary topics of conversation whenever and wherever townsfolk got together.

Slim, being quite uninterested in sports and on a waiting list (number three hundred seventy-nine) for an opening at the plant, never learned any of the lingo and therefore found himself almost completely incapable of communicating with those around him. That was okay by him. He didn't want to be like the others. He didn't want to work at the plant, but in a town like that he had little choice. He didn't want to waste his weekends in front of the tube either.

Instead, he spent much of his time in his room or, if the weather was nice, in the backyard, reading thick books in which he learned of distant places and people who had done exciting things. He knew that one day he, too, would be one of those people, but it sure wasn't going to happen if he stayed home.

"If I am destined for greatness," Slim thought to himself that gray summer's day, "then what I need is adventure. A great sea voyage to a faraway land. Someplace where the meals don't come out of a box or a can, and where entire conversations can pass without the terms 'point spread' or 'split shift' being used once."

It was in that faraway land—any faraway land at all—that his destiny awaited. He could feel it.

Again, he wasn't sure what that destiny would entail, exactly. He might open a chain of penny arcades or Big & Large clothing stores. He might become a subtle and profound tap dancer (the greatest the world has ever seen!) or write an epic novel about how life in a factory town really blows. Who knows? He might even slay a dragon or a giant, should he ever come across one or the other. Whatever it turned out to be, whatever he did on the other side, he knew it would leave him a very wealthy and famous man. Most important of all, all those kids who made fun of him in school would see his name in the papers and wish they were him.

So with a small bag, a crisp twenty-dollar bill in his pocket, and his parents' blessing (to be honest, they were kind of relieved to see him go, the mopey lazybones), Slim booked passage on a grand sailing vessel called the *Humperdink,* set to depart for various ports of call on the other side of the world.

The members of the crew mostly left him alone, which was a relief to Slim. It wasn't that he was snotty or arrogant by any means. He just didn't deal with people all that well. He was especially glad to be left alone during the first three days at sea, which he mostly spent puking over the side of the ship. He hadn't figured on that. Even though he'd grown up so close to the ocean, the closest he'd ever come to being on a ship was at the county fair ten years earlier, on the kiddie boat ride (and even that had made him queasy).

He was almost at the point of wondering what kind of horrible mistake he'd made when the seasickness finally passed. Soon he was quite comfortable wandering about the deck, looking at this and that, and staying out of everyone's way.

One afternoon, Slim was sitting in a deck chair with a fishing pole. A Styrofoam cooler rested on the deck next to him.

He found himself fishing quite a bit as the voyage wore on. Although he never caught much of anything, he found it to be a relaxing way to pass the hours and think about what great things lay ahead of him. He still had no idea what he'd do to achieve it but assumed it would become obvious once he hit land again.

That afternoon, as Slim was dozing, he felt something tug at his line. Yelping with panic, he gripped the pole as tightly as he could and quickly began reeling the line back in. The fish didn't put up that much of a fight, but to the inexperienced Slim it represented the greatest battle between man and fish the world had ever known.

Finally, ten minutes after the first tug, Slim pulled up a four-pound sea bass.

The first odd thing that Slim noticed was that the fish was wearing glasses. The second odd thing was that it could talk.

"Hey!" the angry sea bass shouted as well as it could around the hook lodged in its mouth. "What the hell you think you're doin' there, smart guy?"

Not knowing what else to tell the talking fish, Slim answered, "Um . . . fishin'?"

"*Fishing,* he says," replied the sea bass. "Oh you're a sharp cookie all right, aren't you?"

Coming to his senses a moment later, Slim realized what he had on his hands.

"Why," he said, "you're a talking fish!"

"Two for two there, Isaac Newton. Yeah, fine, I'm a talking fish," the sea bass said. "And I could talk a hell of a lot better if you took this goddamn hook out of my mouth."

"Oh. Sorry," Slim said, grasping the fish with one hand and carefully removing the hook.

"Thanks," the fish said, flexing his lips to see if any major damage had been done.

"A fish that can talk," Slim thought to himself, "must surely be magic. And a magic talking fish must surely be a good omen for the adventures that lay before me! I can't let him get away, or he might take his blessing with him."

So Slim, thinking quickly but not having read that many fairy tales, picked up a small club, bashed the fish over the head, and dropped it into the Styrofoam cooler. "There," he said with satisfaction, "now his magic will stay with me."

Almost immediately after the lid came down on the cooler he heard a frantic shout from one of the sailors. Slim looked to see what the hubbub was all about and saw the helmsman pointing off the starboard bow. Peering across the water, Slim saw the fast-approaching armada.

"Hard astern!" he heard the captain shout. But it was no good. The enemy ships were approaching too quickly.

As they drew closer Slim could see that there were at least twenty of them, each much smaller and swifter than the *Humperdink*. Each of the ships, in fact, seemed to be an exact miniature replica of the *Humperdink,* as if they'd been built from the same plans, but at one-third scale.

It soon became apparent that attempting to outrun them was futile. Slim dropped his fishing pole, grabbed his cooler with the dead magic fish, and retreated to the safety of his cabin as, one by one, the identical enemy ships zipped in close and fired a volley from their cannons. Each took one or two quick shots, which struck home more often than not, then veered quickly away to make room for the next.

The battle raged for many hours, the air filling with deafening roars and the smell of gunpowder, as Slim cowered down below in his cabin, taking occasional fearful glimpses out his porthole.

While the blasts from the tiny ships did little damage individually, the cumulative effect was devastating.

Before night came that evening, the *Humperdink* had been blasted to pieces, and most of what little was left intact sank to the bottom of the sea.

Much to his surprise, Slim somehow found himself floating in open water, essentially unhurt.

"I'm still alive," he said with great wonderment. Taking a look around himself, however, it was clear that none of his beloved shipmates could reasonably claim the same thing.

Realizing he had to do something if he wished to remain in his present state, Slim paddled amid the flotsam, gathering together broken and charred bits of planking, lengths of torn rope, bobbing canisters of fresh water, and anything else he could find.

Then, working as quickly as he could while treading water, he began to lash the planks together. Before long (and again much to his surprise), he'd constructed himself a sturdy and seaworthy raft. It was large enough to hold him and whatever supplies he could grab from the passing waves. He'd even salvaged a small sail, which he raised in the middle of the raft.

Slim knew nothing about sailing but figured the sail couldn't hurt. And, sure enough, it soon caught a brisk prevailing wind and he continued on his journey across the sea. It wasn't quite as comfortable as the *Humperdink* had been, but it was better than being dead, he figured. Taking inventory, he believed he had enough food and water with him now to last the rest of his trip, so long as his trip didn't extend any longer than a week or so. Sadly, his magic fish had gone down with the carcass of the ship. Yet perhaps, he hoped, he had absorbed enough of its magic to make it worthwhile.

"Guess we'll see," he said to himself, as he tore open a candy bar from the captain's private stash and shoved it in his mouth.

Exhausted from his efforts and all that had happened to him, a well-fed Slim lay back and slept quite soundly.

While he slept Slim did not notice as the first shark fin sliced out of the water and began circling the raft. Or the second or third or fourth either. When he awoke the next morning, however, it was pretty hard to ignore the dozen or more sharp dorsal fins sweeping in smaller and smaller circles around him.

"As long as I'm up here, I'll be more than safe."

A moment later the first shark broke from the pack and dove beneath the raft, where it took a passing nip at one of the dangling bits of rope holding the raft together. A second shark followed suit. Undoubtedly they would have preferred the lively morsel up above, but they'd be content with bits of rope until something better came along. And if things kept up this way, that wouldn't be too much longer.

As each shark dove and bit at the rope, Slim couldn't help but notice that the raft he was so very proud of was seeming a bit less sturdy than it had the night before.

Soon the outer planks began to split apart from the others. Slim didn't dare try to retie them, what with all those damn sharks about. All he could do was wait it out and hope they got bored. Little did he realize that sharks, blessed as they were with brains the size and complexity of wood screws, never, ever got bored.

Slim watched in growing terror as, plank by plank, his raft grew narrower. As the boards began to drift away, he saw his food and water supplies splash back into the sea, only to be torn to pieces by other marauding sharks who'd recently joined the party.

Refusing to give up hope—his destiny was awaiting him, after all—Slim snapped off his makeshift mast and began jabbing it at each shark as it drew close enough. There was nothing else he could do.

Much to his surprise, that did the trick, and after a while all of the sharks had decided to look for food in less annoying waters.

Sadly for Slim, by this time he was left only with a single plank, the waves having carried everything else far away. He clung to the plank as if his life depended on it (which of course it did).

"Well," he concluded as he began to kick his feet in what he presumed to be the general direction of land, "at least I'm still alive. That's the important thing." He was more determined than ever now, after all he'd been subject to, that he reach his destination and receive his glorious reward. He'd make those little knotheads from Spengler Memorial High jealous yet.

Slim paddled and paddled without food or water or sleep for the next several days. He could see no land in any direction, had seen no other ships, had no idea where he was or where he might be headed, but still he paddled on because he was alive and because great things awaited him.

When the sun was high and bright on the fourth day following the trouble with the sharks, Slim felt the water swell beneath him.

"That was odd," he said.

He stopped kicking, fearing at first that it might be another group of sharks homing in on his unprotected legs. Looking quickly around, though, he saw nothing.

Sighing with relief Slim resumed his kicking, still holding tight to the board.

Just then he felt a shadow cross his face. Looking up, he saw the enormous, flat tail of a whale break the surface of the water and rise slowly and majestically into the air directly in front of him. Higher and higher it rose, and Slim estimated that the fins of the tail must span thirty or forty feet across, easily.

Never having seen such a thing before except on *National Geographic* specials Slim, quite awestruck, stopped paddling again to witness one of the great wonders of nature first-hand.

Only as the massive tail began its descent back toward the water did Slim notice that he seemed to be directly in its trajectory.

"Holy crap!" he screamed, before letting go of the plank for the first time in four days and flailing desperately away.

The tail crashed down with an explosive *smack*, not only onto the water's surface but on the plank as well, before submerging once again. The waves caught Slim and lifted him high into the air before dragging him deep below the surface and spinning him about three times. At last his head broke water again and he could draw a ragged breath.

Quite shaken, Slim tensed his weary muscles, expecting the whale to reappear at any moment, perhaps even swallowing him whole, Jonah-style.

Nothing happened, and all was silent once more, except for the sound of the wind rippling the waves.

"I'm still alive!" Slim thought, a bit more astonished than those previous few times. He was dazed, certainly, having been knocked for a bit of a loop, but he remained essentially unharmed. Hungry, thirsty, and exhausted, yes, but still not seriously injured.

He scanned the surface of the water, searching for his plank. It seemed hopeless, the force of the whale's tail having most certainly shattered it into a bazillion pieces. Still he looked. He wasn't the kind of man to give up hope on a mere assumption. He would not be deterred.

Five minutes later he let out a whoop as his eyes finally saw what they were looking for, and he swam toward it.

As he drew near he stopped to tread water. With two fingers, he carefully plucked from the surface of a passing wavelet a thin piece of wood no more than two inches in length. It was nothing but a toothpick, he noted, but it was all that remained of the plank that had kept him afloat these past several days. And that plank had been all that was left of the raft that had kept him out of reach of the sharks. And that raft had been all that was left of the ship that had carried him away from that stinking, rotten little town and toward his destiny.

"I'd much rather have that magic talking fish," he said, "but if a toothpick is all I've got, then a toothpick will have to do."

He held it aloft toward the heavens and screamed, *"I'm still alive!"*

Slim clutched the toothpick tightly in his fist and began swimming once more.

Believe it or not, Slim Slinneanach is still bobbing around out there in the ocean to this day—even though all that remains of the toothpick at this point is a painful splinter driven deep underneath the nail of his right index finger. It's not really clear how that one happened, but so long as he still had even a tiny piece of the *Humperdink* with him (no matter how painfully), Slim was absolutely convinced he was going to be all right.

He was kind of an idiot that way.

These Children Who Come at You with Knives

During a quiet period of the last century, there existed a bustling seaside village known to its inhabitants as Happyland. The name, if you can believe it, wasn't simply some cheap ruse concocted by a shady real estate developer or a group of drunken Vikings. The people who lived there really were quite happy. The climate was sunny and cool most of the year, the town itself quaint and almost absurdly picturesque, and the local economy (boosted primarily by the picture-postcard industry) had left the residents comfortably well off with plenty of leisure time. Moreover, with everyone so gosh-darn happy and thus not much interested in shooting or clubbing one another, crime was almost unheard of.

Yes, they had it awfully good in Happyland. The folks lucky enough to live there knew it and were quite proud of the fact. The news from across the rest of the country may have been full of strife and violence and bad feelings, but over there in Happyland things were mighty fine indeed.

"Good day!" strangers said to each other on the street.

"And it certainly *is* a good day!"

They didn't butt in line at the drugstore and they held doors for one another.

It was almost enough to make you puke.

Then out of the blue one day the residents of Happyland began to notice something. It was quiet at first, something they could look at on their way to work then immediately forget. But as time went on it became impossible to ignore.

There were strangers in town. Not the typical tourists who flocked to their charming village all year round to stay in the bed-and-breakfasts and eat muffins at the genteel sidewalk bistros before going home, no, these newcomers were staying, and there seemed to be more of them every day.

Most seemed to be children, or at least much younger than the town's average inhabitants.

Not that they didn't seem as happy as everyone else in Happyland, for they were certainly very happy, always smiling and speaking in gentle, peaceful voices. Sometimes they even broke into spontaneous dances on the sidewalk, or gathered in the park to play strange musical instruments and sing songs in a language the Happylanders couldn't understand.

The first thing that made these interlopers stand out was their clothing. Instead of the cleaned and pressed suits and dresses you found on most of Happyland's populace, these visitors dressed more often than not in torn and dirty rags, sometimes roughly stitched together from odd bits of colored cloth, often looking as if they'd been rummaged out of other people's trash. Something about them just seemed *dirty,* and most of them smelled as if they hadn't bathed in quite some time. They had long, greasy, tangled hair and usually didn't even bother with shoes, walking through the streets and into local businesses with their bare and soiled feet.

But you know, that wasn't such a big problem to the people of Happyland, who prided themselves (along with so many other things) on their live-and-let-live attitude. They had it very good, after all, and tried not to look down their noses (too much) at those who didn't.

No, that wasn't the problem. The problem was that these newcomers didn't really seem to do anything or live anywhere. What the people of Happyland had, they had because they'd worked hard for it, and worked hard to maintain it. Now here these smelly, hairy creatures had shown up who seemed to be living freely off the efforts of everyone else who put in a hard day's work. They clogged the sidewalks, asked passersby for handouts, made the parks wholly unpleasant spots to visit, and stank the place up but good. Worst of all, they didn't seem to care. They didn't care that they did not have jobs so long as they could get handouts. They didn't care that they looked like they'd been rolling around in the mud most of the afternoon. They took no pride in those things the Happylanders held most dear. They were slothful, coal-eating layabouts who did nothing but sing awful, cacophonous songs, take drugs, drink cheap wine, and sleep and have sex in public places. It was all quite mortifying.

Suddenly, for the first time ever, the Happyland Police Department had something to do apart from looking for lost purebred dogs. There were complaints from distraught residents who'd awakened in the morning to find twenty or thirty of these things camped out in their backyard or digging through their trash cans. More unheard of still, the comfortable home of a Happyland family was burglarized by one of these lowlifes who was (it was claimed) looking to get enough money to buy more illicit mood-altering drugs.

A month or two after it became clear the problem was only getting worse and that these ruffians had no intention of going away, a local newspaperman referred to them in an editorial as "Creepy Crawlies." The term stuck, and soon whenever you heard one of the original inhabitants of Happyland mention the Creepy Crawlies, you knew he wasn't talking about silverfish.

Something had to be done about the Creepy Crawlies, the people decided. They wrote to the mayor and held community meetings. There were calls for some kind of referendum or the passage of some new laws that would make the Creepy Crawlies go away. If something wasn't done, the tourists would stop coming. But no one could think of how to properly word a law that wouldn't affect the tourists or the townsfolk as much as the Creepy Crawlies themselves. They couldn't very well say "if you look like this, you must leave our town immediately"—they were, after all, a very liberal, tolerant, and culturally sophisticated people, and that sort of overarching judgment call might reflect badly on them.

They were stymied, and while they continued to hold civilized public meetings to discuss possible solutions, outside on the streets the Creepy Crawly population continued to explode with each passing week. You couldn't walk out your door to go to work in the morning without having to step over a few of them. It wasn't known if they were sneaking in from outside Happy-land or breeding like crazy within their own ranks. Whatever the case, it was way out of hand. And as their numbers continued to increase, Happyland was becoming less, well, *happy*.

One day, a city councilwoman by the name of Nancy Vertigo saw a small item in one of the major metropolitan newspapers she read every day. (Reading papers from big cities made her feel more well informed, cosmopolitan, and righteous.)

She had no idea that Creepy Crawlies were a problem outside of Happyland, but apparently they were. Even if they were called by different names, the description was unmistakable—sloppy, hairy, lazy, drug-addled, and sex-crazed.

That in itself wasn't what caught her eye, however. The story in question reported that the town of Duckwater's Creepy Crawly problem—they were called "Filthies" over there—had recently been solved with the help of a mysterious stranger known only as "Chuck."

This enigmatic Chuck character, the story reported, appeared out of nowhere one day wearing a strange, ornately woven vest and playing a guitar. He looked like any of the other Creepy Crawlies at first, but he seemed to have a special way of communicating with them. It was almost as if he had a kind of psychic power over these smelly youngsters. They followed him everywhere and seemed to do whatever he said. And sure enough, with a little encouragement and a modest cash offering from local officials, one day Chuck strolled out of town still playing that guitar of his, with all the Creepy Crawlies following close behind. They hadn't been seen or heard from in Duckwater again.

"What we need is this Chuck character," Nancy Vertigo thought. "He can take care of this problem lickety-split."

The next morning she brought the story to the city council members and suggested they try and contact him and ask for his help. A motion that they do this as soon as possible was passed unanimously with very little debate. It just made sense, is all.

"But . . . how are we supposed to go about finding him?" a cigar-chomping councilman asked after the vote was taken. "I mean, I'm all for it, you see, of course I am, but I wonder how you intend to track down some guy known only as Chuck? What are we gonna do, take out an ad?"

"Perhaps," Nancy Vertigo suggested. "Or we could contact the mayor of Duckwater and see if he knows anything. It would be a start, anyway."

This course of action was also approved quickly and unanimously. And just in time, too, as in the previous days the increasingly aggravated inhabitants of Happyland had begun venting their frustration directly upon the Creepy Crawlies—intentionally stepping on their prone bodies, refusing to hold doors for them, spitting in their general direction, even aiming for them with their cars. Never in the town's history had Happylanders been known to express such violence toward anybody, and certainly not on such a wide scale. In the past, if you decided you didn't like someone—though there was rarely any reason for that—you simply didn't invite him to your backyard barbecue. That was the more civilized thing to do. You didn't go *stepping* on them, for goodness sake. This recent marked increase in assaults and rude behavior on the part of Happylanders was unconscionable.

On the morning she had intended to put in a call to the mayor of Duckwater, Nancy Vertigo awoke to a strange noise from outside. It sounded like a hundred people were singing one of those awful songs the Creepy Crawlies liked so much—except this time around, all the voices seemed to be blending together so perfectly that she could finally understand the words.

Always is always forever, they sang. *As one is one is one . . .*

For the first time ever, the song—which she'd come to recognize—didn't sound so awful. She put on a dressing gown and looked out her second-floor window.

There, to her amazement, she saw what must have been two dozen Creepy Crawlies walking in neat rows down the street. And leading them all was an unusually short man with long hair and a beard who was playing a guitar. Noticing his brightly colored vest, she knew immediately that it must be Chuck himself. She wouldn't need to place that desperate call to Duckwater after all. Somehow, he must have known that he was needed in Happyland.

She made some excited phone calls, then got dressed, hopped in her SUV, rolled down her windows, and set out to find him.

It wasn't difficult. All she needed to do was follow the sound of the singing voices and the unmistakable stench that arose whenever more than two or three Creepy Crawlies got together in one place.

When she finally found him, Chuck was in the park, surrounded by what must now have been nearly a hundred Creepy Crawlies. Seeing him, she had no doubt that this was the man who could help them with their problem. He would be like a musical exterminator, except that he wouldn't be killing anything.

After she parked her SUV and strolled across the grass toward the crowd, she saw that Chuck was talking quietly to his flock. She couldn't hear what he was saying.

When he caught sight of the approaching woman in the designer pantsuit holding her nose, he stopped talking, raised his hand, and made a small, almost imperceptible gesture with two fingers. The Creepy Crawlies all stood without a word and went away.

Once they were gone, Nancy Vertigo drew closer to him and said, "You may not believe this, Mr. . . . um . . . Chuck, but just yesterday the local government here unanimously decided that we needed to ask for your help."

"I know," he answered. He had intense, almost hypnotic black eyes and a quiet, beatific smile.

"You do?"

"Everyone needs my help, and only I can give it. You might say that every society gets the savior it deserves, so here I am."

"Savior, yes, I see," she replied, coughing a nervous laugh.

She offered him a ride over to the city hall in her SUV but he refused, insisting they walk instead. Being unused to that much walking at one time, she hesitated, but then agreed. If that's what it took, then by god she'd make the sacrifice.

Along the way she explained, "We just didn't know what to do anymore. We're at the end of our rope. The people in this community are very nice and kind and understanding by nature, but these . . . *things*," she snorted. "They just make Happyland so very *ugly*. You understand? And smelly. I mean, just *look* at them. So dirty and lazy. And so *young* too. You have to wonder what went wrong with them. I mean, why aren't they like us? It's a crime."

"Mmm," Chuck said.

"We've tried everything to get along with them. Really we have. But they won't have it. We offer them jobs and they ignore us. We try and show them how to dress for success and they start doing some crazy dance. It's maddening. We just have to find a way to rid our town of this pestilence."

"I understand," Chuck said. His eyes seemed focused on something in the distance.

At city hall, the details of a contract were quickly hammered out. It was quite simple, really. Chuck would rid Happyland of Creepy Crawlies for good, and for his services he would be paid quite handsomely. He made no demands—simply waited for their offer and accepted it.

"When would you like me to get started?" he asked, after marking an *X* on the contract and setting his pen down.

"Oh, as soon as possible, certainly," everyone in the council chamber agreed.

"All right," he said. Then he stood, picked up his guitar, and left the chamber without another word.

Once on the street again, he slung his guitar around his neck and strummed a simple chord. Almost immediately, Creepy Crawlies began emerging from alleyways and gutters and fell in line behind him. As he walked, they arose from doorways and crept out from inside what few abandoned buildings existed in

Happyland. From the parks and the playgrounds and the clinics, they all took to the streets and joined the procession.

Traffic was stopped but, once news of what the hubbub was all about began popping up on the radio, no one seemed to mind the delay. A day of celebration would soon be upon them.

Although elated with the knowledge that the Creepy Crawlies were finally going away, most residents were also astonished at the sheer number of semihuman youngsters who'd been living in the shadows of their fair town. Hundreds upon hundreds of them, it seemed, and they all fell into lockstep behind Chuck, holding hands and singing songs.

> It's time to drop all from behind us
> The illusion has been just a dream
> The Valley of Death may not find us
> Now as then on a sunshine beam.

He made three trips around the village, hitting quiet side streets and major thoroughfares alike, just to make certain he'd gathered all those who may have been sleeping during his first two passes. Then he headed for the city limits.

Now it was Happyland's true residents' turn to take to the streets to watch the plague disappear over the horizon, never to return. When the sound of the singing finally vanished completely, their anticipation erupted into explosive, spontaneous (but very polite) cheering and clapping. At last they'd be able to reclaim Happyland for themselves and for people like themselves. Then they all went back to work.

*　　　*　　　*

Chuck led the Creepy Crawlies deeper and deeper into the endless desert that lay to the east of Happyland. For hours they marched, perhaps even days, without pausing to rest. But as the exuberance of the Creepy Crawlies far outstripped even that of the Happylanders, nobody seemed to notice or care. It was all smiles and dancing and skipping and singing the whole way.

At last the massive and odiferous crowd topped a sandy crest and Chuck stopped walking. Below them, much to their astonishment, they saw even more Creepy Crawlies just like themselves frolicking about the large encampment below. There were ramshackle buildings and beat-up old buses and campfires. Most of the Creepy Crawlies were dancing naked to any one of the dozen impromptu jam bands who'd set up randomly around the camp. For the Creepy Crawlies who'd followed Chuck out of Happyland it was like stumbling into heaven.

Over the course of the next several days the newcomers learned that the camp did indeed have a few rules. Not many, but a few. Since they were Chuck's rules, though, no one found any reason to complain. Their time was their own to do with as they wished, except for dune buggy training (three times a week), firearms training (twice a week), and the mandatory nightly campfire meeting, where Chuck would sermonize.

During the sermons, he told the Creepy Crawlies who'd gathered from all across the land that they were outcast children. Children, he told them, who weren't loved or wanted by their parents or their schools or their churches. They were garbage in the eyes of those people (he called them "pigs"), but they would all find a pure and unquestioning love there in the desert, from him as well as from everyone else in the camp. He also told them how evil and corrupt the cities he'd liberated them from had become, with all the fat greedy businessmen and corrupt politicians who wanted nothing more than to sweep them all under the rug. The desert sky, he told them, was that rug—but like all the dust-balls and fingernail clippings under the rugs in millions of sterile suburban homes, they might be forgotten but they weren't going away. Everyone agreed: those people were fuckers. Then they all took a lot of acid and danced around naked and had a big orgy.

Most of the time, to be honest, nobody really knew what the hell Chuck was talking about. There was a lot of spiritual mumbo jumbo that didn't really hold together all that well. Sometimes he would spend hours explaining the secret encoded messages from God he'd found in the ingredients list on the side of a Froot Loops cereal box. And sometimes he insisted that he was Jesus, Buddha, Muhammad, Lucifer, Frankie Avalon, Captain Caveman, and Yog, Monster from Space all rolled up into one delightful, lovable package.

Baffling as he could be at times, he did provide them with all the food, drugs, and sex they needed, so long as they always did whatever he told them. No one ever saw any reason to refuse.

At his behest, they snuck into nearby towns and stole cars, or rummaged through the dumpsters behind grocery stores for discarded but edible food, or earned money for the camp by working the streets (there was a small but active community of Creepy Crawly fetishists out there, they'd found). They all agreed that money was an evil—but a necessary one. You needed money to pay for those drugs you couldn't grow yourself, after all. At least for now.

All the Creepy Crawlies were as happy as happy could be. And they all knew they had Chuck to thank for it. With Chuck around, there was nothing to be afraid of.

"Chuck has all the fear," they chanted every morning. "We have given our fear to Chuck."

One day Chuck wandered alone through the desert and back into Happyland. Every once in a while he liked to take a peek back at the places where his services had been requested, just to see how honest the people who'd hired him had been. They always promised that they were a peaceful, kind, and giving people and that the kids were screwing all that up for them. They would certainly, they assured him, immediately revert to their peaceful and kind and giving ways as soon as those damned Creepy Crawlies (or whatever folks called them) were out of the picture.

In Happyland, as Chuck had discovered in every other town, this wasn't exactly the truth. Even if they had smiles plastered on their faces all day long, the people were still doing whatever was necessary to get ahead and make more money. They ignored the people among them who were in need. They ate meat and drove pollution-belching automobiles. They were happy, but they were happy with themselves for the wrong reasons, and happy about things that made Chuck want to claw his eyes out.

Things had gotten even worse in Happyland than they had

in those other towns. An awful lot of Happylanders (who'd been forced to keep their more beastly tendencies bottled up in the past) had found that they secretly enjoyed being mean to the Creepy Crawlies. Now with the Creepy Crawlies gone, they went right on being mean to one another, having decided they needed some sort of outlet. As always, without a collective external enemy to be nasty toward, a population that's tasted hatred and bloodlust will turn on itself.

It was evident that, despite all their promises, they weren't very grateful to Chuck at all for what he'd done.

He returned to the camp having decided that if the people of Happyland so easily ignored his first lesson, he'd have to give them another one. This time it would have to be a lesson they couldn't so easily ignore.

Back at the desert camp, Chuck called a handful of his most trusted followers into his tent and explained to them what he had seen, what it meant, and what needed to be done about it. He also interpreted the arcane messages he'd discovered in a passage from a Harold Robbins novel he'd been reading. Then he provided each of them with a long, sharp butcher knife and a length of rope.

That night, while Chuck slept peacefully in his tent, a small, select band of Creepy Crawlies piled into the dune buggies and sputtered off toward Happyland.

It didn't take the Happyland Police Department all that long to figure out who was behind the two nights of unspeakable horror the town had experienced. Scream-filled nights during which seven in-nocent people felt Chuck's wrath. Seven peace-loving Happylanders trying to have a relaxing evening at home made the simple mistake of going to the front door after hearing the doorbell ring. Opening the door and finding no one there, all seven victims stepped out onto their porches, trying to figure out what the deal was.

That's when a group of drug-crazed Creepy Crawlies jumped out from the bushes or from behind the door and blew really loud whistles while waving knives and pieces of rope in the air before running away.

Those damn kids scared the *bejeezus* out of these people!

After interviews with the victims had made it clear to inves-tigators that it was in fact those darned Creepy Crawlies who were responsible, it wasn't hard to trace things straight back to Chuck. His face was well known in town and, in the days prior to the nights of horror, dozens of residents had reported seeing him wandering the streets, scowling a lot, shaking his head, and sticking his tongue out at people. He really should've taken the time to read the small print on that contract he'd signed.

Two squad cars were immediately dispatched to the desert camp to pick up Chuck and bring him in for questioning. On the way back to town, Chuck made it clear to the arresting offi-cers that he'd done what he'd done only because he felt betrayed. He'd done something nice for the people of Happyland but they just ignored it. They'd learned nothing. Their whole kindhearted and neighborly spiel was a lie. They could smile all they wanted, but deep down Happylanders were just as rotten and mean as anyone else.

"Well then, mister," one of the officers said, "you don't like us? Then I guess we don't like you very much either."

And sure enough, as the trial got under way, the general consensus in the media, on the streets, and around office water coolers was that Chuck the Savior, who'd removed the Creepy Crawly scourge from their midst, was really Chuck the Stinkpot who, in spite of all he'd done, didn't know enough to just keep his damn mouth shut and his stupid opinions to himself.

Furthermore, it was also decided, both among the general populace and in the courtroom, that he should be put to death. Not only in order to be rid of him once and for all but also to serve as a warning to anyone else down the line who might try to do anything nice for them, expecting them to learn a little something as a result. They never wanted to see anyone like Chuck in their midst ever again.

Everyone in town—Happylanders both large and small, young and old, rich and, well, richer—came together in the town square on the appointed morning. It was, as always, sunny and cool and nobody took it for granted.

"Beautiful day, eh?" a number of people in the crowd were heard to comment.

In an act of generosity prior to Chuck's execution, the court had offered him the opportunity to share with the people of Happyland any final thoughts he might have. So shortly before ten a.m., after being led up the steps of the gallows, Chuck gazed calmly out over the gathered throng, waiting for them to fall silent. Once he knew he had their full attention he began to speak.

"I have stayed a child while I have watched your world grow up," he spoke in a loud and clear voice. "And then I look at the things you do and I don't understand."

Someone in the mob coughed.

"You people," Chuck went on. "You're just a reflection. You aren't the good guys. You're worse than *we* are."

A small murmur of discontent rippled through the crowd. This wasn't what they were expecting. They were expecting him to say that he was really, really sorry for what he'd done and that he would never do it again.

"And you can't fake on me," he continued. "You can't fake on me because I am your children. I'm what you made of them. These children who come at you with knives—they're *your* children. I didn't teach them. *You* taught them. I just tried to help them stand up. The people out there at the camp—the people you call Creepy Crawlies—they're just people that you didn't want, people that were alongside the road, people that their parents had kicked out, so I did the best I could, and I told them that in love there is no wrong. But these are just a few. There are many more coming right at you. They're gonna yell *booga booga,* and some of them might curse, and one or two might try and trip you so you falls right in the mud. And you won't like it one bit, believe you me."

"Liar!" someone from the crowd screamed. "You're a lousy, stinkin' liar!"

Everybody else was pretty sore about what he was saying too.

"You're just naughty!" a woman shouted.

"Naughty and a very bad person!" an older man added, waving his cane in the air.

Others yelled similar things.

Chuck seemed to take it all in stride. This is what he'd come to expect from people.

"I'll tell you another thing," he said.

"Oh, I think we've heard quite enough," the mayor said, stepping forward. He nodded at the hangman. "Let's get on with this."

As the hangman raised the noose to slip it around Chuck's neck he noticed something peculiar. It was a scar, or a crease or a paper cut or something, that seemed to go all the way around Chuck's neck. He reached out absently and, picking at it, saw that it seemed to be loose. In fact, with a little fiddling, he was able to wriggle three fingers up under the skin of Chuck's throat.

Chuck said nothing. He simply stood there quietly, staring into the crowd. He was smiling a patient smile.

Forgetting all about the noose, the hangman jerked his hand upward, ripping the latex mask clean off Chuck's head with a wet, hollow *schlup*. The force of the gesture combined with the hangman's surprise sent the mask hurtling high into the air, before it arced and fell into the stunned crowd.

Gerard the gnome—who, as it happens, had no real fear of water after all and could hold his breath for an outrageously long time—stood on his platform shoes, grinning out at the bewildered, bloodthirsty crowd. (Can you imagine that? It may sound cheap and contrived but that's what really and truly happened. It was Gerard all along. Honest.)

Gerard's grin began to stretch and distort into a scowl, the black eyes squinting, the muscles of his face convulsing.

Individual memories of the foulest possible kind spread through the gathered townspeople like a brushfire, no matter how young. Useless cruelties, tortured pets, abandonment. Shrieks and howls of shame and horror filled the air as Gerard began to wiggle the stumpy fingers of his bound hands at them.

"Up the winding mountain . . ." he began, but the crowd had already started to scatter in every direction, stepping on the fallen and shoving those who hadn't fallen yet. The only thing each of them knew at that moment was that they had to get away, no matter who was hurt in the process (so long as it wasn't them). Grown men screeched as they threw small children out of their path and teenage girls clawed at the faces of the elderly.

Those near the back and around the periphery thought they had it made, but unbeknownst to them quietly, stealthily, as they'd been gathering for the hanging, the Creepy Crawlies—who now numbered in the tens of thousands—had crept back into Happyland and surrounded the town square completely, waiting for just this moment.

No matter which way they ran, which way they turned, townsfolk came face to face with more Creepy Crawlies. And this time the Creepy Crawlies didn't blow whistles and run away. This time they used those knives of theirs—as well as their axes and forks, chain saws and golf clubs, tire irons, sawed-off shotguns, croquet mallets, zip guns, grenades and two-by-fours wrapped in barbed wire, hatchets and corkscrews. Ropes, too, and a few other things you might not otherwise expect.

"I thought he was just speaking metaphorically!" one man was heard to scream at no one in particular, moments before a Creepy Crawly caught him across the throat with a rusty machete.

As the streets of Happyland grew slick and dark with the blood of townsfolk, Gerard snickered, chewed through the ropes that bound his hands, removed his platform shoes, and descended the wooden stairs of the gallows.

He strolled calmly through the ongoing savagery and carnage, dodging the occasional severed hand, flying kidney, and bouncing eyeball. He figured his first stop would be the mayor's mansion, just to see if he'd need to replace the wallpaper

"Yes," he thought, "it sure is good to be king."

And you better believe that he lived happily ever after.

Not too many other people did, though.

THE END

Acknowledgments

No book is created in a vacuum, and so I would like to thank the following people for their continued help, encouragement, and inspiration in spite of everything:

I can't say for sure how my agent, Melanie Jackson, continues to do it, but I sure am glad she does. She's the best.

Sarah Hochman, my editor, is without question one of the wisest, funniest, and most rational editors with whom I've ever worked.

My dear friend Don Kennison is more than a top-notch copy editor (though he is that)—he has an unusually sharp and wide-ranging mind, and we share far too many obsessions in common not to get along.

I couldn't be happier or more proud to be working with all three.

Thanks are also due Arne Svenson; Joel Fotinos; Ken Swezey

Acknowledgments

and Laura Lindgren; David E. Williams; Germ Books and Gallery; Carly Sommerstein; George and Janice Knipfel; Mary, McKenzie, Jordan, and the late Bob Adrians; Philip Harris; Daniel Riccuito and Marilyn Palmeri; Derek Davis; Erik Horn; Brad Parrett; Bill Monahan; Tito Perdue; Brian Berger; Ryan Knighton; Mike Kenny; Luca Dipierro; Richard Dellifraine; Magus Peter H. Gilmore; John Strausbaugh; Alex Zaitchik; Mike Walsh; TRP; John Graz; Linda Hunsaker and Dave Read. I would also like to thank Bobby Beausoleil for providing the sound track.

Special thanks are due Homer Flynn, for his invaluable editorial suggestions.

Something well beyond special thanks is owed to the extraordinary Morgan Intrieri, who deserves a big chunk of the credit for this book.

Morgan has been involved with the creation of these stories since long before the first word was written. She suggested the central ideas and plotlines which became "World Without End, Amen," "The Boy Who Came to His Senses," "Toothpick," and "These Children Who Come at You with Knives." She also made invaluable editorial suggestions during our countless discussions about these stories as they were being written. There's not an entry here that she hasn't contributed to in some specific and important way.

These stories, and this book as a whole (together with so many other things I've written), could not have happened without her insight, intelligence, humor, patience, and sharp eye for detail. In the very truest sense, she is this book's co-author. I am deeply indebted to her, and love her very much.

About the Author

Jim Knipfel lives in Brooklyn, where he is not welcome in family-friendly establishments.